Also by Faith Baldwin
in Thorndike Large Print

HE MARRIED A DOCTOR
GIVE LOVE THE AIR

NO PRIVATE HEAVEN

Faith Baldwin

NO PRIVATE HEAVEN

Thorndike Press • Thorndike, Maine

Library of Congress Cataloging in Publication Data:

Baldwin, Faith, 1893–1978
  No private heaven.

  1. Large type books. I. Title.
[PS3505.U97N6 1986]   813'.52   86-5688
ISBN 0-89621-712-4 (alk. paper)

Large Print edition available through arrangement with
Holt, Rinehart & Winston.

Cover design by Abby Trudeau.
Cover illustration by Deborah Pompano.

THIS FABLE, CONCERNING A BEAUTIFUL PRINCESS, HER CRUEL FATHER, HER WICKED STEPMOTHER, AND HER INEVITABLE PRINCE CHARMING, IS DEDICATED, VERY INAPPROPRIATELY BUT WITH LOVE, TO TWO YOUNG MEN WHO WERE FORCED TO BECOME REALISTS WHETHER THEY LIKED IT OR NOT. . . .

PFC. HUGH H. CUTHRELL, JR.

AND

SEAMAN, SECOND CLASS,
STEPHEN CUTHRELL

1

Abby came down the stairs quietly; her feet crept, but her heart ran. She kept telling herself, as she had all morning, But you're absurd . . . you're twenty-two years old, and have your full growth. He can't lock you up. He can't put you on bread and water just because you want to go swimming . . . it's so *stupid* to be afraid. He knows you're afraid and that makes everything worse . . .

She reached the landing where the stairs turned, and a picture window looked out over the Berkshire foothills. All this little world was tender and green with spring. She could see orchards, foaming up in rose and white. She knelt for a moment on the wide window seat and looked out, eager as a child. It was late May, unseasonably warm, with leaf and blossom hurtling into bloom as if it were their last time, their final opportunity and they must make the most of it.

She heard her father's voice downstairs in the hall. From its direction she knew that he was standing by the fireplace beneath the Holbein portrait. She did not hear what he said, but a woman's voice reached her clear and high, gushing like a swollen brook. "It's such a *privilege*," cried the voice in italics, "I have always *longed* to see the Wallace collection."

Norman Wallace said, without enthusiasm or conviction, "It will be a pleasure. Shall we go into the library, for a moment?"

The voices receded. Abby went to the railing, and looked over the stair well down into the hall. It was empty, save for the heavy furniture, the benign and intellectual portrait gravely looking down.

She held her breath, and released her hold on the polished wood. A door opened and a young man walked into the hall. He was smoking a cigarette, he wore tweeds, he looked casual and at home. Abby said, "Craig?"

Craig Emerson looked up and saw her standing there. Her heavy hair, pale, burning gold was bound in metallic braids about her small head. Her face was anxious and constrained. She asked, "What's going on?"

Emerson shrugged. He said, "Some woman from New York with an introduction . . ."

Abby came down the rest of the stairs. He

thought, She walks better than most women dance. He said, smiling at her, a pleasant young man with an attractive irregular face, "What in the world are you clutching? Don't tell me you have taken up knitting!"

I might as well, she thought, knit one, purl two, when I'm not going to galleries or working on the book. Aloud, she said, "It's a bathing suit . . . I mean, in the bag . . ."

She had the bag, green, and rubber-lined, over her arm. She wore a tweed skirt in faded pastel checks, a thin sweater, and on her small feet scuffed saddle shoes. The routine uniform of girls all over the country. But she did not look standardized. Nothing could standardize her.

She had reached the last step, and Emerson walked across the hall and stood there leaning on the newel post. He asked, "Where are you going?"

"To the Duncans'," she told him, "it's a swimming party."

Emerson whistled soundlessly. He said, "Your father doesn't like the Duncans."

"He doesn't know them," she said, instantly on the defensive: "he's met Mrs. Duncan only once or twice since she came here."

"Does that matter?" Emerson inquired.

"I suppose not . . ." she added. "Anyway, I'm going."

9

"You rate it," said Emerson. He looked at her with pity and pleasure; pity because he was sorry for her and could do, he believed, nothing about it: pleasure because she possessed so unique a beauty. "It's pretty grim for you," he added, "cooped up here . . . with your father, the collection — and me."

His voice rose a little, as if he had asked a question. Abby looked away from him. He had been a part of their household for a number of years . . . The son of a distant cousin whom Norman Wallace had taken straight from his university. He was intelligent and useful — and also, because of his eyes, unacceptable to the army.

Emerson took off his shell-rimmed glasses. His eyes were brown and very nearsighted. He said, "You'd better scat. I hear someone coming."

But it was too late. The library door opened, and the woman's exclamatory voice followed Norman Wallace into the hall. He shut the door, cutting off all sound, and looked toward his daughter and Emerson. He raised his eyebrows a little, and walked toward them. He said pleasantly:

"I thought I heard voices. I was just about to send for you, Craig. I thought you might take Mrs. —" he hesitated, trying to remember the negligible woman's name — "Mrs. Evans through the gallery . . ." He added, "I wondered where you were, Abby."

His brief nod dismissed Emerson, who looked at Abby a moment, shrugged, almost imperceptibly, then walked obediently to the library door, opened it and vanished.

Abby felt lost. It was not a new sensation. She held the green bag a little tighter as if that might help her. Her father asked softly: "You are going out?"

Abby drew a deep breath. She came down the remaining step and looked up at her father. She said, "To the Duncans' for a swim and luncheon."

"The Duncans," he repeated reflectively. His voice was quiet, very cool. He was a tall gray man; gray hair, gray eyes, gray suit. He added, "I don't approve of Mrs. Duncan, Abby. I'd rather you didn't see as much of her."

She said, "I haven't seen her much . . . just at Red Cross. Earlier in the week she asked me if I would come to swim today . . . she's having a few people . . ."

He asked, "Whom is she having?"

Abby moved her shoulders. She said, "House guests, I suppose, and her son —"

"Has she a son?" inquired Wallace pleasantly. "I didn't suppose she'd found the time. . . ."

"He's been discharged from the army," said Abby doggedly. "He's up for the weekend."

"Do you know him?"

"No," said Abby. She felt her nerves creeping, like ants. She knew that the color rose under her pale, delicate skin. She was suddenly, terrifyingly aware of the weight of the house about her, solid, inescapable . . . a big stone house built by her grandfather . . . a house filled with massive furniture and fine paintings and objets d'art . . . A house dominated by her father.

"I see," said Wallace. "Come over here Abby, a moment. I shan't keep you long."

She followed him to the fireplace and he sat down on an old bench, the cushion faded to a soft glowing rose. Abby stood before him, as a child stands. He did not ask her to sit down beside him. He went on:

"Who else will be there?"

"Oh, people," she said vaguely. "Val Stanley . . . I think Mrs. Duncan mentioned her."

A look of distaste shadowed her father's controlled face. He said, "I have known Val since her childhood. She isn't exactly the type of young woman I would select as your intimate."

Despair came like a fog, it made her voice husky. Abby said, "I've seen very little of her since we were children – I'm not making an intimate of her just because we are both

12

asked to swim in the Duncan pool."

"She's a — model, isn't she?" asked Wallace indifferently. He went on, "You can telephone. You can say, with truth, that I have an unexpected luncheon guest and therefore you must remain."

She said, low, "I've accepted. . . ."

"Well," asked Wallace, with some amusement, "what difference does that make? A great many engagements are broken every day, for quite valid reasons."

Abby said stubbornly, "I want to go!"

Her heart hammered. It was ridiculous standing here, arguing, rebelling. Why? Because she wanted to go swimming . . . and her father did not wish her to go. Again, why? Because he did not wish her to go anywhere, meet anyone?

Surely this was unimportant. How much easier it would be to say, "Very well," go back upstairs and put away the green bag and its contents — a purse, a lipstick, a compact; a bathing suit, a cap, a flask of sun oil. Easier to come down again, having changed into the sort of frock of which her father approved . . . to join him and his visitor in the gallery; easier to sit at the head of the luncheon table and listen, and be what was expected of her: her father's hostess, his unofficial private secretary in some matters, his quiet, well brought-up daughter. . . .

But it wasn't unimportant. It was vital. It was spring, even the cold gray stone of the old house warmed to spring. She was twenty-two. Next year she would be twenty-three. It was a matter of simple arithmetic before she arrived at an age when spring would no longer matter. Her father had reached that age many years ago. He was seventy-three.

She twisted one long hand within the other and steadied her heart with a deep breath. She steadied her voice. She said, "I'm going . . ."

Her father rose. He said wearily, "Very well, But I prefer that you do not go unescorted. I'm sure that Craig would be glad to go with you."

She said, knowing the objection idiotic, "He wasn't asked."

Her father said carelessly, "My dear Abby! Half the people who go to establishments of the type maintained by a woman of Mrs. Duncan's informality are not invited. You know that as well as I."

He went to the library door, opened it and spoke pleasantly, "Could I see you a moment, Craig?"

Emerson shot out of the library, closing the door, looking from one to the other. Wallace said with a faint, frosty smile:

"Abby's going slumming. It would be" — he

hesitated deliberately — "pleasant for her if you went along."

"To the Duncans'?" inquired Emerson, startled out of his usual composure. "Well, of course, Uncle Norman, if Abby wishes. . . ."

She said, with a spark of anger, "Does that matter?"

Wallace said smoothly, "I'll take over Mrs. Evans . . . as Morris is in the city." He looked at Abby. "I hope you'll be back in time to take some dictation before dinner. Say, five?"

He nodded at them briefly and went back to the library. And Emerson said gently, "I'm sorry, Abby."

"It's all right," she said.

He said, "I'll just be a moment. I'll dig up my bathing trunks and join you."

She said, as he started up the stairway, two steps at a time, "I'll wait in the car."

But, as he disappeared, she did not move, for a moment. She stood quite still, hating herself because she was shaking. But a small flame of triumph warmed her . . . as it always did on such occasions. They were rare but they had occurred. At long intervals, she had her way, if never important; at least people who didn't know wouldn't think it important.

She looked at the heavy library door, closed against her. She thought, Father . . .

It seemed impossible to her, even after all these years that you could begin by loving someone as much as the child Abby had loved her father, yet by the time you were twenty-two there was no love left, none at all, only fear.

Fear of what?

Of his eyes, amused or angry but always glacial; of his voice, controlled, without feeling; of his words, which said so little and meant so much?

She shook herself a little, as if dispelling an enchantment, and walked, with her head high and her unconscious grace, into the small morning room opening from the square hall. It was entirely French in feeling and décor, faded colors, gilt, delicacy . . . Over the fireplace, another portrait, this one of her mother.

Abby stood looking up at it. She often came here to look at the portrait and wonder about the woman who had sat for it. She had never known her. She had been an infant, sleeping, eating, crying, comically smiling, engrossed in the business of comfort and survival, when her mother died . . . at twenty. Twenty, two years younger than Abby, and she had known marriage and childbirth and death. What sort of woman was she, the daughter of Pennsylvania Dutch farm people, whom Wallace had discovered in a little town playing the organ in a country church . . . ?

She had been painted wearing a stiff blue brocade gown, very period, almost costume. It was a fine, mannered portrait. Behind her, an indicated artificial landscape, dark, somber; in her lap, just touched by her long hands, a sheaf of lilies. She looked down at them, her face still and beautiful, her heavy hair hanging to her shoulders, caught up in some fashion so that it belled forward, smooth, glowing gold.

Perhaps the artist had been a little in love with his subject. There was tenderness in the small mouth, the flesh tones, the broad eyelids. Perhaps he had been afraid to paint what he saw in the eyes, for they were nearly hidden. But Abby knew what they were like. She saw them in her own mirror every day . . . long eyes, almost aquamarine in color, under the heavy white lids . . .

Craig spoke, just behind her: "You are very like."

She started perceptibly. She said, "I didn't hear you come."

"I'm sorry." He touched her shoulder, quickly, and a little shiver went through her because it was pleasant to have the trivial weight of his hand on her flesh, even fleetly, laid there in affection, in, perhaps love.

But she couldn't love Craig, she reminded

herself, she did not dare.

He asked, "Isn't it time we were starting?"

They went out of the morning room and the portrait was no less lonely. It did not matter to the painted face nor to the painted hands touching the stiff immortal flowers who came into this room or who left it . . . it did not matter to Susanna Wallace whether her daughter came there and looked at her, and implored her silently, or questioned her, to no avail, or whether strangers came and exclaimed over her curious beauty, as they had when she had lived, or whether the man who had been her husband came and looked at her with satisfaction because he had desired that she remain as she had been, at eighteen . . . and, she had so remained, in a portrait.

2

Abby's car waited outside, a small coupe. May waited too, on the sweep of lawn, the meadows beyond, the driveway, bordered thickly with elms, the crazy quilt of stone walls, the foothills beyond. May waited in the sunlight and the light, warm breeze. . . .

Abby drove, over Emerson's perfunctory protest. She liked to drive, to feel power under her hands, power she could control, guide, suppress or encourage. She drove well, very smoothly.

He said, leaning back, "This is all right . . . I'm grateful to Uncle Norman . . ." The avuncular title was a concession to informality, easier to handle than cousin. "But I'm sorry if I've spoiled your party."

Abby laughed, "How could you spoil it before it happened? Besides, I'm glad, after all, that you came. Of course I don't like being told I must be chaperoned. But perhaps I'm a little scared."

"Will you never get over your shyness?" he asked gently.

"No ... yes ..." She shook her head, "I'm not shy, really," she said.

"No," he agreed, "not with the thousand and one pilgrims to your father's house, not at the head of his table or walking through the gallery, not in auction rooms or commercial galleries ... But sometimes with me, and always with your father, and inevitably with young people ..."

Craig signed. He understood her, up to a certain point. He was also in love with her, he had been for a long time. He had watched, with bitterness, when she had fallen in love with someone else; and had observed, with compassion but a certain comprehensible gratification, when Norman Wallace had entered the picture — a charming picture, all youth and growing awareness and delicate reactions — to destroy it with complete finality. But he thought, What have I to offer her? Not, at any rate, the one thing she wants.

For the one thing which he believed Abby wanted was escape. He could not offer that, for he could provide no means. All he knew Norman Wallace had taught him ... patiently, and with thoroughness. All he knew was art, as exemplified by the Wallace collection, one of the great private collections of the country. Wallace was grooming him against the day when the curator of the collection, Jay Morris, grew too old to be of much use, and would retire upon his ample savings, and perhaps, write a book. They all wrote books. Without Norman Wallace, without the collection, Emerson was lost, and knew it. Not that there weren't places where his special aptitudes would command a living and more: commercial galleries, other private collections, art museums. But there was still much to learn, and he would be a fool to throw his opportunity away . . . a worse fool to antagonize his benefactor. No, if he could persuade Abby to marry him, she would not escape.

He asked conversationally, "What sort of woman is Mrs. Duncan?"

Abby said, her eyes on the curving road:

"She's wonderful, I think, in her own way. She has tremendous vitality — a little like a steam roller, perhaps. When she comes into the Red Cross rooms, everything's stepped up. She can work rings around most of us there. Some resent her of course, she hasn't been here very long and you know what the old-timers are like —"

"Two years, I think," said Emerson, "or a year and a half. I forget. The old Barstow place had been boarded up for years, until she bought it.

How old a woman is she, what does she look like?"

"I don't know how old," said Abby, "it's hard to tell; so as to that and what she looks like, you'll have to find out for yourself."

"Do you know Duncan?"

"No . . . I've seen him, once or twice, at the station."

"Is he her fourth husband," inquired Emerson, "or her fifth?"

"I wouldn't know that either," said Abby, smiling.

"A woman," commented Emerson, "who has had four or five husbands! Honestly, Abby, after the second, it doesn't make much difference, does it? It seems so greedy. I am not at all astonished that Uncle Norman doesn't approve."

Abby said, "It doesn't seem to me that her marriages are our business."

"Perhaps not. There's a son, I believe," said Emerson, "back from the wars. Medals and all that sort of thing." His voice was frankly envious. "Are there other children?"

"I don't think so," said Abby. "If so, she hasn't mentioned them to me. Only this one – Barry Lambert."

She was silent remembering Madge Duncan's vivid face, her quick voice, saying, there in the

Red Cross rooms, her hands competent and occupied, ". . . you must meet my son, darling. If I do say so, he is really something. Of course," she had gone on briskly. "I was more in love with his father than with any of my subsequent husbands. Barry's father was my first, you see, and occasionally a first experience is romantically perfect, so all others seem a little lacking . . ." She had added practically, "Who knows how long it would have lasted? Barry's father died when Barry was quite small."

"I should think," said Emerson judicially, "that he would hate all this — the son, I mean."

"All what? The Barstow place?" Abby looked at him in amazement. "But it's a nice old house," she said, "the typical white farmhouse. The swimming pool was the Barstow's idea, when they made so much money . . . and, of course, the terraces and the stables. I went there several times when I was quite small. I liked it. . . . whatever happened to the Barstows?"

"God knows," said Emerson, "what does happen to people who make money suddenly and then lose it, just as suddenly? They jump out of windows or crawl into obscure flats . . . The place was mortgaged to the hilt, I understand. I dare say Mrs. Duncan got it for the first six bars of a song, from the bank . . . When did the Barstows leave? I don't remember them, I wasn't here then."

"About twelve years ago," Abby said.

"I didn't mean," said Emerson, "that Lambert would hate the place. I meant, all the various stepfathers . . . a title of sorts, if I recall the gossip at the time she came here . . . English, I think . . . and before that a banker . . . and now Duncan, whoever he is. Of course she can afford them," he added carelessly, "as the money's hers. She was an Elson."

"What's that?" asked Abby lazily. "A breed of cats or marsupials?"

She was different, away from the stone house. Emerson had very rarely been with her, away from the house. Yes, she was quite different.

He said, "Old settlers, you know the type . . . real estate, big properties, apartment houses, hotels, various city realty. Like the Astors . . . I suppose times and taxes have eaten into the original holdings but they are solid enough." He looked at her sidelong. He said, "Lambert should be quite a catch."

Abby said indifferently. "Maybe someone's caught him . . . I first heard about him from Val Stanley. I ran into her in the village, shortly after he returned from abroad. It was some time ago. She was quite articulate on the subject."

"Oh, Val," said Emerson. Everyone in Fairton knew Val . . . a native product, local girl makes good in New York.

She asked, "Don't you like her?"

"My dear," said Emerson, "I'm scared of her
. . . all that sultry façade and her picture on
magazine covers, too."

"How do you know it's a façade?"

"I don't," said Emerson promptly, "but I'm
not going to find out. Hey, don't miss the turn."

The Duncan sign was there, on the left.
There were big oaks on either side of the driveway . . . and flowering shrubs. A robin flickered
by and an early oriole.

She said, conscious of her trivial triumph –
was it trivial? – "I'm beginning to wish we
hadn't come . . . but I'm excited about it, too."

He put his hand over hers on the wheel. He
said, "You poor kid. If I could give you the
world with a fence around. . . ."

She was again aware of the pleasure his touch
gave her, yet it was almost an impersonal
pleasure, such as she took in the impartial
shining of the sun. She said quickly, definitely:

"But, Craig, I wouldn't want – the fence."

3

Earlier, by the pool, Madge Duncan sat in a long chair talking with her son. She was a thin woman, very brown, with dark-red hair skillfully touched up. She had little beauty but great animation. She wore a peasant-type frock designed for a fourteen-year-old and it did not look grotesque. From a distance she looked like a fourteen-year-old, long thin brown legs and arms, a small scrubbed face, brightened only by her wicked black eyes and her lipstick. Her house guests had not come down from the house as yet. The big cement pool, oblong, painted blue, and flagged around the rim, was rippled a little by the breeze. Fresh spring water poured into it from the open mouths of incredible cement fish. There were chairs and umbrellas all about and directly back of Mrs. Duncan, a small cabana, with dressing rooms, shower, and a portable bar.

She said, without complaint:

"I haven't seen much of you, Barry."

He was a very big young man. His hair was dark red, as hers had been when she was younger. His eyes were black as hers. But his face was differently shaped, and his mouth. His mouth was like his father's, the modeling of his skull and his rather long nose.

He said, "Believe it or not, I've been busy."

"You needn't be," she said. She had always spoiled him, she wanted to spoil him now.

"I know." He grinned at her. His teeth were very white, and a little uneven. "Don't worry, monkeyface."

She did look rather like a monkey, an attractive, intelligent monkey. She knew it, and didn't care. She said, hesitantly for her, "I'd like you to be happy."

"Lovely, maternal thought," he said, smiling. "I am . . . I'm out of that mess," he said, "alive. I even have a job . . . complete with a paneled office, a beautiful blonde secretary, not at all dumb, and three telephones which kindly refrain from ringing."

He had entered, after his return from the hospital, the offices of the Elson Estate . . . competently managed by a gentleman who had been in them since, practically, time immemorial. He drew a salary . . . more than adequate for what he was expected to do as an apprentice, learning estate management . . . And he had, besides, the small income left him by his father, William Lambert.

His mother said uneasily, "David tells me you insist upon collecting rents. . . ."

"Well," he said, "I was getting nowhere faster than the speed of light. So I hollered. So they sent me out with one of the underlings to collect rents. I was baffled. I thought all your rents arrived in envelopes, represented by slips of paper drawn upon solvent accounts. But it ain't so, darling. The East Side is the Mecca of all the New Yorkers from Iowa, Illinois, Brooklyn, Connecticut, and Los Angeles . . . but it is also the home of thousands of people who live in walkups and whose rent is collected in cash, weekly. You meet interesting characters, when you ring doorbells."

She said, "I'll never understand why you moved — you were perfectly comfortable where you were."

Barry grinned. His mother had performed a minor miracle. Upon his return from the wars he had found an apartment waiting for him . . . a small correctly furnished bachelor establishment in a good apartment hotel with an excellent address. His mother had said, "I though you'd like this. . . ." She knew how he felt about living in her duplex . . . a co-operative affair which she had owned for years. Not that he didn't like Duncan, as well, or better, than his predecessors, not that his mother's gang didn't amuse him. But he had been on his own for a long time.

He stretched and Madge saw the long ragged scars across his ribs. They had faded but they were still very noticeable. She shivered, turning her eyes away.

It had been no trouble to dispose of the hotel lease, housing conditions being what they were.

"But," she demanded, "why move to that rabbit warren?"

"I like it," he said. He regarded her tolerantly. "And you don't even own the dump. Although you do own some near by."

Madge had been in Barry's flat several times. It was furnished after the rather haphazard tastes of its original tenants, who had moved to the West Coast. It was a little shabby-arty, with sagging bookshelves and bad modern paintings, with gloomy green curtains of an indefinable material, and a wide old couch in the living room, covered with an India print. The bedroom was undistinguished and the kitchen a haven for cockroaches. Also, it was on the top floor. You rang, the door opened with portentous clickings, and you walked up.

She said, "Well, you've always had independence."

She had given him that, after the early years of dragging him to and from Reno. She hadn't interfered, no matter how she felt. When he had enlisted as a private – and at that time, perhaps, wires might have been pulled – when he said bluntly he wasn't interested in OCS . . . she hadn't interfered. She hadn't meddled in his various love affairs. How serious was he about Val? she wondered. She didn't especially like Val, but then she wasn't going to marry her. Was Barry? Madge would hold her tongue if he did. She wouldn't say, Darling, the word is old hat but it's still a good one . . . gold digger. At least, I think so. Not that you aren't attractive, in yourself.

She loved her son, but she had loved a number of other men, and not maternally.

She said, "I suppose I've been a rotten mother."

"The world's worst," he agreed cheerfully, "but a lot of fun . . . There's Val . . . and Bob."

Val Stanley and Robert Duncan came around the windbreak of pines and waved at them. Duncan was a big man, he looked impressive. He wasn't but he was amiable and easygoing and comfortable. The tall girl beside him was very dark. She looked as dangerous as an unfenced precipice. Black hair, brown eyes, a clear skin, a full, very red mouth, a miraculous figure. She wore a striped toweling robe over a white bathing suit.

"Hi," she said.

She was staying at the house for the weekend. She came over and sat down beside Madge. She said, "The Lawsons are just up, they'll be along. Pete Carstairs is riding, someone told me. Who else is missing?"

She smiled at Barry, whose pulse accelerated. Last night, out on the terrace . . . damnedest girl he'd ever seen, one moment in your arms, the next eight feet away. He remembered giving her the cigarette and her unrevealing face briefly illuminated by its flame. He remembered her voice, consciously low and deep. "Well, *really*, darling," she had said, "you didn't return from the war yesterday. You've had time to adjust yourself and control your reactions!"

He couldn't believe her. What man would? The way she looked . . . if there was anything in that. She looked like embers, smoldering. If you took her in your arms . . . But you did, and she was as light and evasive as ashes . . . and as cool, as ashes long burned out.

Madge said, "I've asked Abby Wallace."

"Good Lord," said Val, "Abby? But she won't come, she never comes."

31

"She said she would."

"Who is she?" asked Barry.

Robert Duncan grunted, and regarded with annoyance his stepson's flat stomach and lean waist. Duncan's stomach was slightly frilled over the waistband of his trunks.

He said, "She's part of the Wallace collection."

Madge said, "Barry doesn't know the Wallaces."

Duncan said, "But he knows about the collection."

"Stamps?" asked Barry politely.

Madge said lazily, "Don't be stupid. Art, of course . . . all kinds, but principally paintings. Now and then he lends some of them to a museum. His father started the collection. It's as famous as any in the country."

"Hell of a lot of money tied up in it," said Duncan. "Not that he's had to worry. He's never done anything *but* collect. Occasionally he sells, at a huge profit. But not often. Has a curator, or whatever you call 'em, one of the cleverest men in the country . . . and agents all over the world. Or had, before the war. He still lives in that dreadful house the older Wallace built, but this one built the gallery . . . I got in there once, last winter, when I came up to see about something here on the farm. I used to know Morris, the custodian or whatever, and ran into him at the tavern and he dragged me over. Wallace wasn't too pleased. For a guy who collects he isn't very hospitable."

Val said, yawning, "He's a sweet old thing, really."

Barry spoke to her directly. "Anything male would appeal to you."

"Thanks," she said, unsmiling.

Duncan lit a cigarette and went on:

"He has bombproof vaults and all that sort of thing. The more valuable paintings were housed there until recently. Now they are back where they belong, I suppose. But I saw plenty at that. I believe he's left them to the Met. I wouldn't know."

"How old is he?" asked Barry. "Anything over forty's old to Val."

"I resent that," said Duncan, "and, moreover, I don't believe it." He grinned a little. He enjoyed watching Val cast her little net. Barry was a pretty big fish. Also, he swam well.

"He's over seventy," said Madge promptly.

"Saw the girl once," said Duncan; "she's remarkable."

"Girl?" asked Barry, incredulous. "How could she be?"

"Norman Wallace," said Duncan, "was fifty when he married, for the first time."

"My mother," said Val, "says it caused an earth tremor in Fairton. He threw a party for his bride. She wore a Grecian robe and played the harp . . . or maybe an electric organ."

"No kiddin'," said Barry.

"Farm girl," said Val, "from the hinterland. He went somewhere looking for a painting in someone's attic and found her, instead."

"The daughter," said Duncan doggedly, "is a raving beauty."

Val shrugged. She said, "I suppose so. She used to come here summers, with a governess . . . her father was usually in Europe. Sometimes she joined him there. The rest of the time she was in Fairton. She had a little pony and cart and they used to drive through the town. I knew her, all of the native kids," said Val with acidity, "used to be washed, braided and instructed within an inch of their lives and go up to Stone House for a party, every summer. It was pretty shattering. The rest of the time, she was away at school."

"Sounds rugged," said Barry.

Madge made a motion with her hand. She said, "I hear someone . . ."

Craig Emerson and Abby rounded the windbreak following the manservant who had been with Madge since Barry's birth. Madge's eyes widened and Val's narrowed. The men rose, and

Madge rose. She said, "Abby, I'm so glad you came."

Abby said, a little breathless, "I brought" — she hesitated — "my cousin," she said firmly as if the very distant relationship put the status of an uninvited guest on a surer footing. She made the presentations, smiled at Val. She said, "Hello, Val," and Val nodded, and looked at Barry. He was frankly staring, looking down from his great height.

Madge said, "You know my husband . . . and this is my son." She added, "Barry Lambert."

Barry took Abby's hand. She didn't know why, as she had not offered it. It was long and beautifully shaped, almost boneless in his grasp. He asked, puzzled, enchanted, and because of the enchantment, which had possessed him at the exact moment he had first seen her, a little alarmed, "I couldn't have . . . but I *must* have . . . where in the world have I seen you before, Miss Wallace?"

Madge said, "Let go her hand, for heaven's sake . . . and let the poor child sit down."

She sat down herself, on a glider, and motioned Abby to sit beside her. Abby said, "I don't think you have seen me, Mr. Lambert."

"I have," he said, "I know it. I —" he smiled — "I couldn't forget, you know."

His mother said lightly, "Darling, I didn't

35

know you went to art museums or looked at re-productions or prints."

"Good God," said Barry, affronted. "I don't."

"That's where you've seen her, however," said Madge serenely, "hanging on a wall . . ."

Craig Emerson laughed. He had liked Madge Duncan, on sight. He asked, "Have you ever heard of Botticelli, Lambert?"

"Please," said Abby, discomfited, but Val laughed. She said, "It must be such a bore, Abby. But I suppose it happens, all the time."

"Could someone let me in on this," asked Barry plaintively, "or am I the only one who isn't nuts?"

Val said patiently, "Abby looks like the women Botticelli painted. Even a beautiful un-cultured hunk of a man like you should recog-nize that, darling." She looked at Craig Emerson and asked, "Isn't that so, Craig?"

Emerson grinned. He said amiably, "Yes, but it's a shame to tag her with it."

Madge touched Abby's cheek briefly with her brown hand. She said, "We're embarrassing her." Her tone was lazy but her glance at Val was sharp, and Val was quite aware of it. She said instantly, "Ah, but it's only envy — for the Botticelli women are out of this world."

"I'll say," said Barry. He looked at Abby and grinned. He asked "Would your father permit me to come up and look at his Botticellis some time?"

His regard warmed her, it was a tangible warmth, she felt and welcomed it. She said lightly, "I've never cared too much for the Botticellis . . . they look as if they had low blood pressure . . . and a little neurotic."

But she did look like them, the sweet shape of her face, her mouth, small and full, the floods of yellow hair which she never cut because her father abominated short-haired women. Her eyelids too . . . but her chin was shorter, more pointed.

Madge asked, "You're swimming, aren't you, Abby? Let me show you your cubbyhole in what we laughingly call the cabana. It was once a farm cottage, I understand, and the Barstows moved it here."

She rose and Abby with her, and they went into the cabana. Barry sat down on the ledge. He whistled, as if he had been holding his breath. Bob Duncan spoke to Emerson, "How about a drink," he inquired, "before you swim? I think it's too early myself, despite the warm weather. I'm strictly a calendar man. When do you think we'll hear about an invasion? I can't get Barry to hazard a guess . . . he's infuriating."

Val sat down on the ledge, her robe discarded. She was distracting in the white bathing suit. She slid close to Barry. Her beautiful legs dangled and she touched a tentative toe to the blue water. She said, "It's cold."

"Could be . . ."

She said, "There's a dance at the Country Club tonight, the season's first, if you have enough gas. . . ."

"Let's stay home," said Barry, "and discuss what makes you tick."

"It might be fun," she agreed. She sighed, looking across the water at the low hedge, beyond which were gardens. They were somewhat overgrown now, there was only one outdoor man on the place except for the chauffeur and the colored boy in the small stables. She said, "I used to envy the Barstows, terribly."

"Why," asked Barry, "the Barstows, for the matter, anyone?"

She said, "I lived where my parents do now, in the village. White house, needing paint, front yard, back yard. Father moved into Fairton from the farm, when he married. He was a carpenter."

"Sure," said Barry, "I know . . . what of it?"

"Nothing," said Val, "except that he still is, with a little real estate on the side since his brother went into the business of showing properties, after people began coming here from New York. I remember," she said, "how I hated

Abby Wallace and those terrible parties and her fat pony and hag of a governess, all long teeth worn on the outside."

"Well," said Barry, "the governess has gone, bridgework and all, the pony's probably dead, and Abby's grown up."

"That's what you think," said Val. "She looks the same, a beautiful little girl in a picture frock, different from all the rest of us."

"I didn't see the picture frock."

"It's the *effect*," said Val impatiently. "The sweater and skirt can't disguise the effect. And she holes in here . . . Good Lord, if I had her opportunities. . . ."

Barry said lazily, "Seems to me you've made the most of yours, sweetheart . . . a flat in town, photographers, pinup girl – I ran into your pinups all over, in the oddest places, and on the most unusual walls."

"You did?" said Val, and flashed into life. She added, "I do get letters from men overseas . . . lots of them, awfully sweet."

"Oh, sure," said Barry, "they're awfully sweet, all of our boys." His tone rasped like a file and Val looked at him and away. She said, "I'm sorry, Barry."

"What for?"

His stepfather came out and silently handed Val a drink and Barry another. Barry's hand closed around the cold smooth glass. He had had a drink; two, in fact. He didn't want this one. He set it down beside him on the flagstones, aware of the sun and the world's remoteness, of the provocative body beside him, aware, and remembering something Vining had said to him before H hour, that time: "If we ever get out of this," he had said, "I'm going to concentrate on having a hell of a good time for the rest of my life."

There'd been no rest . . . except the ultimate, for Vining. But Vining had given Barry his life. He had tossed it at him carelessly, with half a grin, as if he said, Here, take this to remember me by.

Barry heard his mother's voice and Abby's, and rose. He saw the Lawsons appearing and Pete and the little group form, while his mother made the presentations. He waited until it was over and then he went up to Abby, touched her arm and drew her aside. She wore a black dressmaker suit, very plain. The sun was brilliant on her heavy braids. She carried her head so well, yet it seemed as if it must droop from the weight of the hair, on the round, slender throat, long and flawless.

"Someone give you a drink?" he asked.

"I'd rather wait," she said.

He thought, She's the loveliest thing I've ever

seen, and the strangest. She was new to him. He could not pigeonhole her. He did not know why she looked as she did, controlled and vulnerable at one and the same time. The curve of her cheek was as young as the year, but her clear regard was too grave. She smiled often, she laughed, he thought, seldom. There was a shadow in her eyes.

He was an intensely curious young man. Half of Val's attraction for him was that he was unable to make up his mind about her.

He took Abby's hand, casually, held it, swung it a little. He suggested, "Let's go over to the deep end, shall we . . . and jump in, together . . . if you can't swim, it doesn't matter."

She said, "I can swim."

She felt his hand, she was terribly aware of it. It was not like Craig Emerson's hand on her own, familiar, and comfortable . . . it was very disturbing.

Barry Lambert was disturbing. She tried to make a little small talk. She had been trained to small talk, by teachers and governesses, just as she had been taught to run a household, with the help of a housekeeper, speak good French and Italian and passable German; just as she had learned to dance and ride, and sit at the head of a table; as she had learned shorthand and typing in order to be of use to her father; as she had learned other things . . .

Her father had discovered her intelligence when she was very young, and the fact that she was as absorbent as a sponge. It had pleased him to teach her the things in which he was interested. He had not discovered her beauty until she was eighteen.

"Come on," said Barry, and drew her to the diving board. "Jump — don't be afraid."

4

But she was afraid . . . not of the blue water, warmed by the sun, reflecting the faded, striped umbrellas, the pine shadows, the spring sky, reflecting Val's breathtaking figure as she stood on the ledge some distance away, putting on her dark glasses, talking with Craig Emerson . . .

Nor of her own reflection, the white and gold and pale rose coloring accentuated by the somber bathing suit . . .

But afraid of the sudden excitement in her blood as she looked up at Barry's lean face, the features sharply defined, the black eyes warm and amused . . . a very masculine face and, despite the warmth and amusement, unrevealing.

"Well," he demanded, "what gives?"

She said suddenly, "You hang in art galleries too."

"Baby," said Barry with resignation, "are you nuts?"

She asked "Hasn't anyone ever told you?" Her

eyes slid over his astonishing physique, halted briefly at the scars. She said, "My father would recognize you at once . . . that is, in a bathing suit . . . not that Adam wore one."

"My good child," said Barry, "you look almost human with a touch of otherworldliness, but you are addicted to double-talk."

She took her hand from his, and immediately wished she had not. She said, "Michelangelo's Adam, Mr. Lambert . . . you should make a point of looking it up some time," and dived, swiftly, cleanly, into the cool, fresh water.

Barry watched her rise to the surface. She had put on a little while before, the tight white cap. None of her hair was now visible. Her face, no longer dominated by the weight and burning color, emerged with a startling bone structure, delicate and strong.

She shook her head and laughed. She asked, "Are you coming in?"

Barry dived. He was conscious that Val and Emerson were still standing there, some distance away, watching; that his mother was watching too, from the lawn chair.

He came up, close to Abby and touched her smooth wet arm. He said, "Race you to the end of the pool . . . and then let's pray for lunch. I could eat a wolf, and," he added, "there are several present."

"Cannibalistic?" inquired Abby, surprising herself.

Barry grinned. He said, "Time will tell. Remind me at the very first howl."

He won, of course, although she swam very well. They reached the shallow end and stood up, and he took her arms and lifted her to the ledge. She took off her tight cap and the pins slid from her hair and it began to uncoil. Barry said, staring, "Let it down . . . I haven't seen a girl with long hair since —" he paused, scowling into the sun — "since my grandmother died. She was seventy-six and hers was long and thick too, but white. And she was quite a girl at that."

Abby said, "Certainly not," and was not referring to his deceased grandmother. She looked around for the pins, and felt Barry's hard hands on her head. He said softly, "You have a nice little skull."

He liked the feel of it, in his hands, through the masses of hair. He found the other pins and the braids uncoiled and fell over her shoulders. The ends were roughened into curls. He said, "Well, that *is* something."

Val said, just behind them. "Very pretty. Wasn't the name Rapunzel?"

Someone shouted, "Lunch" and Barry rose and pulled Abby to her feet. She said, visibly embarrassed, "I'll be back in a moment," and went off toward the cabana conscious of what she considered her absurd appearance, in the long childish plaits. If she loosened them from bondage, her hair would hang like a sheet of gold to her waist. She smiled, self-consciously, at Madge Duncan and the others as she passed and murmured something unintelligible.

The cabana was empty. She went into the small cubicle where she had undressed. There was a built-in bench, a little dressing table, a mirror, and the usual assortment of oils, lotions, powder, towels.

She was shivering, and had brought no robe. She looked at the guest robe hanging from a hook on the wall and shook her head. She took off the wet suit. She had a beautiful, fragile-boned body, very narrow through the waist, with small high breasts, and rounded hips. She was long-legged, perfectly proportioned.

She looked at herself, almost blindly, and flushed. She had not been conscious of her body for a long time. She took a towel, dried quickly, splashed toilet water on her neck and arms, and dressed. She rebraided her hair and wound it around her head, leaned forward to draw the lipstick firmly over the exact curves of her mouth . . .

When she returned to the others, luncheon

was being served from the hamper that had been brought down from the house: sandwiches, aspics, hot coffee, iced tea, whisky and soda; you had your choice. Barry was shaking cocktails for those who preferred them, at the bar. And Madge Duncan asked, "Dressed so soon, Abby . . . aren't you going in again?"

Abby said, "I don't think so. But it was wonderful . . . the first swim of the year."

Val, in her bright robe, stretched out beside Madge, said lazily, "I've often wondered why you hadn't a pool — "

For the price of a pool you could buy a painting. Norman Wallace believed in comfort but had no special leaning toward luxuries in living. Abby had asked him four years ago if they could have a pool and he had responded reasonably that, what with diminishing returns on invested income and rising taxes, they could not afford it. Besides, he had never enjoyed the spectacle of naked young people screaming around an artificial body of water.

She accepted the martini Barry offered, and Emerson appeared, having occupied himself usefully, with a plate of sandwiches, a dollop of aspic and the usual olives and celery. He asked, "Coffee, Abby, or iced tea?" and she said, "Coffee, I think."

When he had gone, Madge said lazily,

"That's a nice boy . . . did you say he was your cousin?"

"Very distant," Abby told her, "but he's made his home with us for some time."

"What does he do?" inquired Madge, who operated on the theory that if you didn't ask you wouldn't be told; sometimes you weren't told anyway but at least you had tried.

Abby said, "Oh, it's not a job you can define exactly." She finished her cocktail and put the glass on a little metal table. Norman Wallace served cocktails to his guests as a concession to their bad taste, but without approval. He drank sparingly, dry sherry before his dinner, and occasionally a glass of wine with dinner. Now and then after dinner, and in great moderation, brandy.

"But he has a job?" persisted Madge. She thought, He's in love with her, of course.

"He's an apprentice, really," said Abby, "in a way. Sometime he'll take over Mr. Morris's position. He — well," she said helplessly, "he does some traveling for father, and interviewing, goes to galleries, and auctions, all that sort of thing."

"You," said Madge accusingly, "what do you mean holing up on your hill? You ought to be out having a very giddy time."

"I ought to be out," corrected Abby somberly, "doing something worth-while."

"Well?" asked Madge.

Abby tasted a sandwich. She said, "My father's not young, Mrs. Duncan, and he needs me."

But he doesn't, she told herself despairingly. He likes to look at me . . . he wants me around. If he could hang me in the gallery he would be satisfied.

When she was small and in boarding school, as she grew up, an odd child, an introvert among hearty extroverts, she had thought, One day I'll be home with my father . . .

Other girls bragged about their fathers, and their mothers; or talked casually, sometimes hiding scars, of divorces — half a year with this one, six months with that; some played one parent against the other, profitably. Abby had only her father. "Why doesn't he come to see you?" they inquired brutally. And she would say stoutly, "My father's very busy . . ." or "My father's in Europe."

Sometimes she joined him, wherever he was. When he discovered her eager, receptive mind, he had been delighted and set himself painstakingly to instruct her. She had tramped for many miles through the great art museums of Europe. On the day following each excursion he expected her to tell him what she had seen, what she had liked, why she liked it.

She had wished to grow up, very quickly, and become indispensable to him. Well, she had grown up and she had no illusions about her usefulness, the secretarial work on the book he might never finish, the occasional mission with which she was entrusted.

Madge said, "Your father sounds damned selfish to me."

Barry appeared with a fistful of sandwiches and a drink. He sat down on the end of his mother's chair and set the glass on the flags. He said cheerfully, "If I were her father I'd be selfish too."

Abby looked at him gravely. She had known very few young men: and only two, well – Craig, familiar, comfortable; and a lad in the office of the law firm that attended to the Wallace business affairs. Thinking of him, she felt a little sick.

"He," said Madge, indicating her son, "has a wonderful line – inherited," she added with complacence, "from me."

Barry regarded his mother with affection. She was crazy as a hoot owl and he didn't always approve her taste in husbands, but he was very fond of her. She gave him his head. She had never tried to devour him.

He said, "Monkeyface, I sometimes wonder how you ever produced such a beautiful, healthy, normal and intelligent specimen as myself."

"Well," said Madge modestly, "it wasn't easy, but I managed. Of course," she added, "I had help."

Barry laughed and Abby smiled, with constraint. Madge looked at her and raised her eyebrows. She said, "We've shocked her!"

"No," said Abby. She was not easily shocked. If she was innocent, she was by no means ignorant. No girl who had gone through the various boarding-school mills could remain ignorant. But her contacts with people like Madge Duncan were few . . . and most of them, through current fiction. She read everything and anything, avidly and without discrimination. Her good taste and common sense were often affronted, and her natural fastidiousness. But she was not shocked.

She was, however, bitterly envious . . . of Barry's relationship to his mother, the easy give-and-take, the complete naturalness, the affection.

Barry said, "Finish your sandwiches. We're going for a walk."

Madge asked, "How do you know she wants to?"

"What difference does that make?" inquired her son, faintly astonished.

Abby felt his hands on her wrists again, pulling her up. He warned, "Don't step on my glass." From the corner of her eye she saw Emerson coming toward them, with the coffee. She said, "But . . ."

"You can always drink coffee," said Barry. "It's in a thermos. It will keep warm."

His tone implied that *he* wouldn't, and she found herself walking away with him. They turned the corner of the tree windbreak, the pool vanished, and the voices receded.

5

He had his robe slung about him, and disreputable slippers on his feet. He said, "My mother likes you very much."

"How do you know?" asked Abby.

"I can tell." He added, "She doesn't often like my girls although she has the good sense to keep quiet about it."

He waited. Abby said nothing. She walked beside him, her head bent. She might have been a thousand miles away. He was interested and impatient. He had thrown her her cue, and she had not taken it. He asked:

"Why don't you say something?"

She said, after a moment, "I have nothing to say."

They were on the other side of the pool now, and she could see it again, the water, the faded colors of the umbrellas, Val's robe, Mrs. Lawson's gray head. The hedge separated them . . . and presently they had turned their backs and were walking through the spring garden, newly, prematurely in bloom.

She said, "This is lovely. I wish we had one like it."

"Don't you?" he asked, astonished.

"No . . . not, since my mother died. Flowering shrubs, of course," she said, "and climbing roses. My father doesn't care much for flowers . . . unless —" She stopped.

"Unless what?"

She went on as if she had not heard him, for it was futile to explain that no flower was as lovely as one Georgia O'Keeffe and no spring morning as perfect as one which Corot had painted. "Besides, we haven't many men on the place . . . just enough for the vegetables and lawns and to look after the trees."

He asked, "When am I going to see you again?"

"I don't know," she said, conscious of sorrow.

"Here," he said, "let's sit down." There was a stone bench here, warmed in the sun. Trees grew at a distance, a hedge enclosed them, and the flowers were sweetly scented. The sun was bright and concentrated, and it was quiet here, except for bird song and the sound of bees . . . everything was distilled, the warmth and the fragrance. It was a drowsy place but the sky and air had a great clarity.

He asked, "What kind of girl are you, anyway?"

Abby said after a minute, "And if I said again . . . I don't know?"

"I'd believe you," he told her promptly. "You're the damnedest —" He broke off. He asked curiously, "Have you ever been in love?"

"Once."

"And?"

She said, "It was a long time ago."

"I don't believe that. Was it Emerson?" He added grudgingly, "He seems pretty regular."

She said, "It wasn't Craig."

Not Craig, of course, but it might have been Craig any time in these last, say, two years . . . sometimes she wished it were. But she couldn't fall in love with Craig, not wholly . . . she did not dare.

"He was telling me," said Barry conversationally, "about his eyes and all that. I don't know why he feels he had to explain, but most of them do. He's damned lucky, that's all I can say."

She said, "You were wounded?"

"Oh, sure," said Barry. "I'm a hero. Medals and such. They make a pretty rattle if you keep 'em in a tin box. . . . Tell me about your other boy friend, the guy you were in love with —"

She said, "I'd rather not."

"Why? Most girls prefer me to Mr. Anthony."

She hadn't the faintest idea who Mr. Anthony was. She said, "There's nothing to tell. Besides —" she looked at him —"are you always so curious and so — personal?"

"Naturally," he informed her. "If you'd ask about me, now, I'd tell you. I lack reserve," he added, grinning, "like my mother. My love life is an open book, if banned in Boston. I'm an interesting character . . . I've ambitions," he said solemnly. "I'm full of plans for the postwar world, at least for as much of the world as I'll inhabit. I even have a job. I'm a solid citizen. No difficult adjustments, no psychosis, not even one little neurosis. You don't have to handle me with tact, patience, and understanding. Look," he asked anxiously, "am I selling myself?"

Abby laughed and he regarded her with satisfaction.

"I wasn't sure you could — more than once a day," he said.

"Could what?"

"Laugh . . . Do you think your father will like me?"

Abby said, "I doubt it."

Barry shook his head. "Must be rugged," he said sadly, "everyone likes me . . . well, practically everyone. Do you?"

She said, and was conscious of a too keen awareness of his nearness to her, his extreme masculinity, "I – think so."

"Make up your mind," he said. "Abby, you're a very strange little person. I watched you today talking to the Lawsons, holding your own with Val – and she's quite a girl, you know . . . a little on the sharp side. I watched you with my mother, and with Emerson. But when you're with me . . . what's the matter?" he said coaxingly. "It's like talking to you through a glass wall."

She said, "I'm a little afraid of you."

"Of me?" He looked blank with astonishment. "Could be flattery," he said thoughtfully, "and, could be something else."

Abby said, "Yes." She thought, This is a fantastic conversation. But somehow it seemed important to her that it continue, that she make her position clear, if she had a position. It seemed imperative that she and Barry Lambert, who was a stranger to her, understand each other from the outset. And that was foolish, as she might never see him again. And, reaching this reasonable conclusion, she was unaccountably grieved.

Barry leaned back and fished in his robe pocket for cigarettes. He offered her the battered pack and Abby refused. He asked, "You don't smoke?" and then, "Will you tell me why you're afraid of me?"

He put his arm along the bench, at the back, but Abby leaned forward, a little. She said, "I'll try."

It was her habit to be truthful. She had not come into contact with sufficient people to learn that, while honesty is the best policy, it can often become embarrassing and markedly antisocial.

She said, in her clear, rather rapid voice, "I've known very few people my own age."

"That means," he murmured, "men. At the moment I feel half a century your senior. I'm twenty-six, by the way . . . And you aren't exaggerating? You must have gone to school!"

"Several," she agreed, "boarding schools. But I didn't know the girls well."

"Why not?"

She sketched a gesture with her shoulders. "No special reason. I didn't go in for athletics particularly . . . perhaps that was it."

Or for confidences, she thought, after lights, sticky fudge and crumbling saltines, the surreptitious cigarette with the windows open, the letters passed from one hand to the other . . . "a really divine boy . . . he goes to Choate . . ." or Taft, or Princeton, or Yale . . . as the case might be.

He said, "Took all the scholarship prizes, I suppose . . ." and added, "poor kid."

"No," she said, "I didn't. I was only a fair student."

"But there must have been girls," he said, "there always are . . . who asked you home, who came home with you — girls with brothers, big families —"

She shook her head again. "There weren't."

She remembered a hockey team captain — Peggy — Abby had had a terrific crush on her, from a distance . . . just as she had had on Miss Lacey, her Latin teacher, at Mrs. Howard's. She remembered others, later, but mostly Peggy and Miss Lacey because they were the first. Peggy had treated her with casual good humor, she was a senior, a big, handsome, careless girl used to the worship of small fry. Miss Lacey, young and trying to be earnest despite an incorrigible humor, had been very kind. But she had embarrassed both Peggy and Miss Lacey . . . saving her allowance, buying them useless, expensive gifts, votive offerings. . . .

Barry said, "I'm waiting."

Abby looked up, startled for a moment. She had been back at Miss Howard's, the square white school in Virginia, back in the cottage that housed the younger girls. In another moment she would have gone on to Miss Jarrod's, in Central New York, and reached, after that, the secretarial school in Boston. They had all been alike.

She said, "I don't know why I'm trying to explain." But she did know. It was important. It was necessary. "At home," she said, "I had governesses. My father was away a good deal. Sometimes we traveled to meet him somewhere . . . London, Rome, Florence, Paris. . . ."

"Who traveled?"

"My governess," she said, "or chaperon, or whoever it was, and I . . . to meet Father and Jay Morris, and later, of course, Craig."

"I see." He didn't, however; he looked bewildered. "But you didn't travel in a *void*," he argued. "There had to be other people, on shipboard, in trains, in hotels —"

She might have been an eight-year-old, from his tone. She recognized it. She said patiently, "There were, but I never grew to know any of them."

"And now," he asked, "at home?"

"People come," she said, "of course, to see my father and the collection. . . ."

They had taught her to meet them, to look after their comfort, at Miss Jarrod's. She remembered the weekly social hour, with the girls taking turns at receiving, at pouring tea, at making small talk among the visitors. She was no more shy in the rote-learned than she would have been reciting the alphabet, also learned by rote.

He said violently, "It sounds like a hell of a life to me. Did you ever think of getting away? I don't mean by the usual means," he added, "for if I suggested that, you'd look at me and say, 'but I don't know any men . . .' I mean, a job, for instance? Or can't you do anything?"

He looked absurd, scowling at her, but his eyes were friendly; more than friendly. Sudden sheer joy shot up within her like a long-repressed flame. She could not have said why.

She answered, "Of course . . . I speak several languages, I am an excellent secretary, and I can even cook!"

"Well!" he said in triumph. "There's your out. Everyone wants cooks."

Abby admitted, "I would even be useful in an art gallery." The laughter, which had illuminated her face, was extinguished. She said, "I couldn't leave my father." She added, not, "he needs me" as she had said to Madge Duncan, but the exact truth, "he might need me."

Someone was calling. "Barry . . . where are you, Barry?"

It was his stepfather. Barry rose, and Abby got to her feet. She did it better than most women. She looked smaller than she was in comparison to his great height. The birds went on singing and the flowers opened their round petals, and it was warm and hushed and scented. . . .

Barry put his arms around her. He had known her a very little while – Well, that didn't mean anything, he had known other girls for as short a time or shorter, and had put his arms around them . . . laughed a little, and kissed their willing mouths.

But Abby stood quite still except for an inner shivering which somehow communicated itself to him. He did not kiss her but held her, quietly, in the circle of his arms, and presently released her. Yet he was more troubled by this brief contact than he had been by many kisses, given and taken.

He said, "Okay, let's go. . . ."

On the way:

"I'm staying up here for a couple of weeks," he said, "and coming back weekends during the summer . . . I'll be seein' you, Abby. Tomorrow? I'll come to the house. It isn't far, is it? I don't know my way around, yet."

"Just a few miles. But . . ." she hesitated.

"But what?" he asked. "Are you going to be difficult again?"

She couldn't say, But my father would receive you, and see that you didn't return . . . I don't know how, but he'd manage.

She said aloud, drawing a deep breath, feeling as if she were doing something incredibly courageous, "At teatime, then?"

"Long before," he said. And, as he had earlier in the day, he took her hand and held it, swinging it carelessly. He still held it as they rejoined the group at the swimming pool.

The Lawsons had vanished. Peter Carstairs, middle-aged, eligible and wary, was still there, arguing with Madge Duncan. He had wished to marry her before Duncan. He would still wish to, after. He was sure there would be an after. Duncan was watching, amused, and Val and Emerson were swimming again. Val looked up as Abby and Barry made their appearance. She spoke to Emerson a little sharply. She said, "Dereliction of duty, Craig. If Mr. Wallace hears that you let her out of your sight for half and hour, he'll have your ears on a Cellini platter – if Cellini made platters."

Emerson made a face at her, swam to the far end and went up the steps. It was still early in the afternoon and he was enjoying himself. Val was exciting and entertaining, and, even if, as he suspected, she was being amiable to him because Barry wasn't around and she resented the fact, Emerson did not quarrel with her motive. Besides, he liked the easy way in which the Duncan ménage was run, cheerful, pleasant, comfortable.

He looked at Abby and asked, "Coming in again?"

She said, that, no, she wasn't and added that she was sorry but she thought that it was time for them to go.

Emerson nodded and went off to dress and Abby went to sit by Madge and tell her how much she had enjoyed the party.

"Not," said Madge, "a party, exactly. You must come again, you must come and swim every day." She patted Abby's hand. "And tell your father that I'm coming to see him . . . I'd like to see the collection."

Abby said she would tell him.

Barry, sprawled on his face on the flagstones, raised his head. He said, "I'm asked to tea, to-morrow."

"Maybe I'll come too," said his mother, who came and went as she pleased and left her guests to amuse themselves. She added, "It would be marvelous, Abby, if you could lead Barry in the direction of culture. He's never been one for the museum, the opera or," she added, "the ballet."

"Good God!" said Barry.

His mother went on: "But, since his return from overseas, he's gone proletarian."

Barry said, his head on crossed arms, his voice muffled:

"Old hat, darling. It's the proletariat who really enjoy the museums, the operas, and the ballet. You attend because it's smart. They attend because they want to. Where have you been all these years? Ever hear of a place called Russia?"

"You see?" said Madge to Abby. "He spends his days — when he's supposed to be working — prowling around the dingier districts, asking impertinent questions."

"In your behalf," said Barry, rolling over; "collecting your rents."

"And living," said Madge, ignoring him, "in the most dreadful arty little flat you ever saw . . . Top floor, and if you toil up another flight and push open a door, painted blue on the outside, there's a roof with a tree in a wooden pot, two camp chairs, cigarette butts, and all the soft coal in Manhattan."

"A penthouse," insisted Barry; "a poor thing but mine own. You must come up and see me some time," he told Abby, smiling.

"Also," said his mother, "he has joined a political club or something and he threatens to go to night school."

Abby asked, "What for?"

"Don't ask me," said Madge. "Perhaps

he likes the teachers."

Barry sat up and hugged his knees. He said, "I had a lousy education, Abby. I was kicked out of the best schools and it took three universities to give me a degree. Don't you think night school has glamour?"

"It depends," said Val, coming up to sit on a metal chair near Madge, "on the curriculum."

"Now you," said Barry, turning his attention to her, "you might profit by a spot of night school – or wouldn't you?"

Abby was silent, listening. She had made a habit of both silence and listening for a long time. She felt remote again, no part of this particular picture. She watched Val's dark, mobile face, the tilted eyes and very red mouth. This was the sort of girl who understood Barry, who would be comprehended by him. She felt a sharp saddening envy.

Emerson came out and she rose and made her farewells. There was nothing shy about her, speaking the conventional phrases; no lack of poise. She had integral dignity. And besides she had been well taught.

When they were in the car, "Have a good time?" asked Emerson.

"Very."

"I did too. Val, for instance. What a woman. I have seen her only a dozen times, I suppose,

66

and I forget her in between but each time when I see her again she has all the impact of a block-buster."

"She's almost beautiful," said Abby.

"But not quite. She won't wear," said Emerson, "as you will. When you are eighty, you'll still be beautiful."

She was twenty-two; to become eighty would take a very long time. She considered it, without hope.

He said lightly, "What was the idea of vanishing with Lambert?"

Abby said, "I didn't . . . that is, I didn't vanish. We were on the other side of the hedge, in the garden."

"He's all right," said Emerson, "and has, I suspect, more on the ball than you'd imagine at first meeting. I liked him." He paused and added deliberately, "He liked you."

Abby said nothing. He was accustomed to that.

He asked, "You're going to see him again?"

"Tomorrow," she said, and the flame shot through her again and she was warmed by it.

Emerson said, "Well, it's your business, but Uncle Norman won't much like it."

She said, a little wildly, "Why not? There's nothing wrong with Barry Lambert, or his people for that matter. And no earthly reason why I can't ask my — my friends to the house, is there?"

He said, startled, "Of course not; but your father did express himself rather strongly, if you remember."

She said, after a moment, "I remember. But then, perhaps he —"

"What?"

She forced herself to finish, hating her cowardice. "Perhaps he won't be there," she said.

There was another silence. Then Emerson said:

"Perhaps not. He did say something about, he might go to town . . . but it wasn't very definite." He looked at her quickly. "You recall that, I dare say."

She had recalled it, when Barry had said, "Tomorrow?"

Emerson leaned back. He said, "You haven't asked anyone to the house since —"

Since Malcolm . . . four years ago. She remembered the first time he had come, not by invitation, but by command, bringing papers for her father to sign.

She said, "There's always a beginning."

"Worse luck," said Emerson gloomily, "as you know how I feel about you."

She had known for some time. She had been

glad about it, in a way; and in another way, sorry. Because if she ever permitted herself to drift into loving him, through familiarity, through loneliness, then there would be no escape, not ever.

He said, "Last time I spoke of this I said I wouldn't again until you gave me permission. So, I'm breaking a promise. But you would be happy with me, Abby, I swear it. For I would love you, I do love you very much."

Nice to be loved, wonderful to be loved . . . better, perhaps, than loving.

She said gently, "I'm sorry, Craig."

6

On the following day Norman Wallace went to New York with Jay Morris, to attend an auction, and discuss a matter of authenticity with one of the better known experts, and Abby, too aware of excitement and expectation, listened to the elderly housekeeper complain of the shortcomings of a curtailed staff, went for a short walk, transcribed the notes her father had dictated the previous afternoon, and lunched with Craig.

He asked, watching her almost untouched plate, "You seem a little distrait . . . aren't you well?"

"Perfectly."

She had superb health; she looked frail and was very strong.

He inquired, "What's the matter, Abby? I passed the library door about six last evening and heard Uncle Norman's voice. As he rarely raises it, I wondered —"

She said, thinking back to that unpleasant cross-examination. "He was asking me about the – the Duncan family."

"Meaning, I assume, Barry Lambert," said Emerson. "Well?"

"Nothing," said Abby. "He just doesn't like them, quite arbitrarily, that's all."

She was determined not to talk about it. It was a matter of deep humiliation that she could face her father with confidence engendered by reason, and severe self-admonition – Look here, Abby, what in the world is there to be afraid of really? – and then in a few minutes find herself reduced to that fearful inner shivering, her hands cold and her heart hammering in her throat.

She had not told him that Barry was coming to see her. She had counted, almost prayerfully, upon her father's absence. For if she told him, she knew that half a dozen words would reduce her to an abject docility that would take her to the telephone . . . "May I speak to Mr. Lambert, please? . . . Mr. Lambert? This is Abby Wallace. I'm so sorry but I find I cannot be at home tomorrow afternoon, after all."

A double humiliation if something in his reply told her that he had not intended to come.

After luncheon, she worked on the notes. She cleared her desk, in the anteroom of her father's

71

library. She went to the gallery to find Emerson and consult him about a telephone inquiry which had come in from the Coast and left him to deal with it. She changed her frock. It was still very warm. She opened her closet door and after considerable thought selected a shirtwaist dress of pale-green linen, belted in brown suede, and with a little brown jacket.

She thought, I'm crazy. He won't come, of course he won't come.

She was at once unbearably disappointed and relieved.

At a quarter of three she was called to the telephone. She picked up the instrument with apprehension. She said, "Yes?"

"It's Val," said the other voice. "How are you, Abby?" Val's tone was colored with laughter. She went on, "Pete Carstairs and I are about to ride . . . I wondered if we could ride through your place. I remember the bridle paths . . . I wondered if your father would mind? We'd be careful to close the gates . . . We might," she added, "stop by, later, at the house."

Abby said, after a moment. "The paths aren't kept up, Val, they haven't been since the war. My father doesn't ride any more, and I haven't in some time."

"We could take machetes," said Val cheerfully, "and hew our way through. It would be fun, rather. So, if you don't mind?"

Abby said faintly. "Of course not," and presently hung up. She thought, Val knows that Barry is coming here . . .

Well, if she knew, he *was* coming. . . .

He came at three and Abby went to meet him in the drawing room. It was, at any time, an impressive place. He looked at her and grinned. He said, "You didn't expect me, did you?"

"No," said Abby. "Yes. . . ."

"Make up your mind."

"I wasn't sure," she admitted. She asked, "Won't you sit down, Mr. Lambert?"

"Skip the preliminaries," he advised, and glanced around the big room. He waved a brown hand at the paintings on the walls. "This — the collection?" he inquired.

"No," she said, "it is in the gallery. Would you care to — ?"

She thought, Craig will be there.

"Nope," said Barry. "I don't give a hoot for the collection." He looked at her. "Can we get out of here?" he asked, "this place is too big, too —" He broke off. "Outdoors?" he suggested.

She took him through the sun porch, out the French doors. There was a small, rather overgrown terrace here with a barberry hedge that hadn't been clipped recently. The sun was warm and on the branches of an old pear tree beyond the hedge an oriole was swinging, like a flame.

Abby sat down in an Adirondack chair and Barry on the end of a long bench. He said, "You look as if you hadn't slept."

"An unflattering conclusion," she remarked. It was true enough. She had slept wretchedly. Waking, her mind had been made restless by wonder, by fantastic imaginings, she had dreamed, only to wake again. It had been a very bad night.

"I didn't either," he said abruptly, "I couldn't get you out of my mind . . . I suppose you're beautiful," he said, staring at her. "There was quite a discussion about you after you left, between my mother and Val, with my stepfather refereeing . . . I was consulted. I wouldn't know, Abby, I see you differently. Beauty has nothing to do with it. I know that your face, the way you walk, the way you use your hands and carry your head — it's all as familiar to me as if we had grown up together . . . and don't start telling me I've seen you on the walls of art museums. It has nothing to do with a chance resemblance to women long dead and probably idealized," he said, half smiling, "but it has everything to do with us . . . that sense of familiarity as if, finally, I had come home."

She said very directly, "It's foolish to talk to

me like this. You don't know me."

"Who knows anyone?" he demanded. "Who wants to? It's the learning that matters between men and women. You know I'm in love with you."

She flushed. She said, flesh and blood and nerves informed by a most irrational delight, "It isn't possible."

"Of course, it is," he said impatiently. "Do you think that everyone has to go through the preliminaries? I said, skip them. I meant it, Abby." He got up and came to sit on the arm of her chair, very close, too close. "I want you. There's no possible argument. I know it. I shall make you know it. I've fallen in love I suppose a dozen times . . . fun, or not, while it lasted, as the case might be. No scars anyway. This is something else. Last night was pretty re-markable. I wanted to push the walls out . . . the ceiling was too near. I wanted to shout. Morning was an eternity away. I thought, when morning came, I couldn't wait another mo-ment. I'd come at once, and tell you. There's a first time for experiencing anything . . . this was a first time for me. In a way I resented it. Nor is it as unreasonable as you might think, to believe that you feel this way too because any-thing like this can't be for one person . . . one person couldn't sustain it. It has to be shared."

He bent his head and put his cheek against her hair and sighed as a man sighs who has been hurt and knows a lessening of pain.

Abby sat very still. It couldn't be happening, but it was. It had never happened to two people before; yet it happened every day. With one part of your mind you repudiated the thought that anyone else could have experienced this shock of delight, this instinct for surrender; and with the other you told yourself that true lovers had always met and known each other, like this.

"Darling —" he said urgently.

Abby moved away a little. It was the last thing she wanted to do and the first thing she must. Barry straightened up and looked down at her.

He said, "You don't give yourself away, much. I could shake you until your teeth rattled in your lovely head. I think I know what's underneath the surface but I'd like some confirmation." He put out his hand and took hers, lying still in her lap. He said, with elation, "You're ice cold!"

She said desperately, trying to keep her head, "We met yesterday, Barry."

"Yesterday," he said, "tomorrow, a thousand years ago. Does it matter? Do you know why I've never asked any girl to marry me? Because no matter how crazy I was about her, at the moment, I was never certain I could be faithful to her. And I wasn't being noble for her sake. I was thinking of myself, how I'd hate not being faithful and all that went with it. But I could be faithful to you, always."

She thought, I couldn't bear it if you were not; she thought, I couldn't risk your not being, Barry. Aloud she said, "That's — today. Tomorrow you will think otherwise."

"Not any tomorrow," he said. "I want to marry you. Now. As soon as possible." He laughed suddenly. "We have the rest of our lives in which to be engaged," he reminded her. "The important thing is being together."

She said slowly, "The important thing is being *sure*."

"I'm sure," he said confidently, "enough for us both. If you love me. . . ."

"How can I," she asked, "so soon?"

"Is there a stop watch on loving?" he demanded. "This minute, no; the next, perhaps. You're afraid, aren't you? You said yesterday you were afraid of me . . . and you gave me a ridiculous reason. Was it the real reason?"

"No."

"Was *this* the reason?"

After a moment she said, "Yes. . . ."

Barry stood up. He put his arms around her, and lifted her from the chair. They were quite alone, but if a dozen people had been there he would not have cared. He held her close and kissed her. He kissed her again and then put his cheek against her hair and stood there, very still. "This is it," he said, after what seemed like a long time.

She was no longer frightened and she was not rational. She was without thought, mindless. Everything that was right and enduring, everything that was right and transient, in the world went into that embrace . . . the sun's penetration, the sound of birds singing, the spring, the new green, the smell of the earth and growing things, the eternal sky.

He said, "Sit down, there. Let me look at you."

She sat down, gratefully. Her knees were fluid. But her hands were warm now and the color rose sweetly to her throat and face.

Barry stood away a little, and laughed. He said, "When I think I know your face by heart, it alters and I have to learn all over again." He said, "Let's go in and tell your father. . . ."

She said, "He isn't here," and remembering him her mind steadied and became wary, as if it were hunted.

"He will be," said Barry impatiently. "Let's get in the car and go tell my mother."

"No —"

He had not asked her if she loved him, she remembered suddenly, with incredulity. He had taken it for granted. Perhaps she did not. Perhaps this was just . . . release after long bondage, a beautiful but curable lunacy.

He said, "You're going to be difficult. Why? We love each other."

Abby said after a moment, "What makes you sure — of me?"

"I know. Look, Abby, we aren't children. This isn't something that happens after a school dance. We're grown up. At least I am and I assume that you are. This has happened to us both. Some people have more warning, that's all. What's the use of wasting time? I should have thought, I still think, you're the last girl in the world who'd play hard to get."

"I don't," she said. She looked at him, reluctant to make an admission. "Perhaps," she said, "I'm afraid, again."

"Of what?" he demanded.

"A lot of things." She couldn't say, My father. He'd laugh at her, he'd ask, What has your father to do with it? She couldn't say, Of loving you too much . . . because he would answer, That's impossible. But it wasn't impossible. She knew her capacity and her frustration.

They heard voices and Barry swore. He said, "That's Val."

"Did you tell her you were coming here?"

He said, "Sure, why not? She wanted me to ride with her and Pete. I said I had a date. She asked, where, with whom, and I told her."

Abby thought, She has no *right*.

She rose. She said, "Mr. Carstairs is with her. She telephoned me, before you came, to say they were riding and wanted to use the bridle paths." She was walking away from him, around the terrace, to the front of the house. She looked back over her shoulder, and he was standing still, looking furiously angry, looking murderous. And she was aware of terrible pleasure. He resented Val, he resented everyone. He wanted only herself. If it were to be like that always . . . ?

She smiled, secretly, quickened her pace, and called to Val and Carstairs, looking down from their horses, Val superb and self-confident, in her casual riding clothes, Pete looking a little worn around the edges.

"Overgrown was right," said Val; "we couldn't go through. May we come in, Abby?"

Barry had come up and stood frowning into the sun. He said politely, "By all means, ride right in."

"You could give me a hand," said Val.

He helped her dismount and Pete slid off his horse, remarking that he thought he'd walk

80

home. And Val asked, "Is there any place where we can tie these nags?"

The gardener, Morton, was working near by. Abby called him and he came up, dour and incurious, and took the horses and led them off down the driveway to the empty stables.

Abby said brightly, not looking at Barry, "It's time for tea . . . let's go on, shall we? I'll send for Craig, he's working in the gallery."

They had tea in the sun porch, Emerson appearing before the first cups had cooled. The sun porch was the downstairs room Abby had been permitted to refurnish as she pleased, some four years ago. The floor was flagged, and there were many French windows and a fireplace. The furniture, reed and bamboo, was comfortable, the chintzes still bright. There was a big radiophonograph in one corner, plenty of small tables, and ash trays, and a long table for magazines and books. There wasn't a vestige or reminder of the collection here.

They drank their tea. Emerson watched Abby pour hers, put in too much sugar, and drink it as if it were water. He looked from her to Barry who, he thought, was talking too much, laughing too much, and certainly behaving a little oddly. Val and Carstairs had highballs. Barry had refused.

Barry said abruptly, "In the words of the old

cliché, we want you to be the first to know. . . ."

Abby's cup clattered in the saucer. She was perfectly white. She spoke his name, almost shouting, "Barry!" she said.

He went on unmoved, "We're going to be married, Abby and I."

Val flushed a dull red under the olive skin and Carstairs, an imperturbable gentleman, said mildly, "Is that so?" Nothing that Madge's son could ever do would astonish Carstairs, who had known Barry's father and all the Lambert successors. Sooner or later, he thought, Barry was bound to show something of the determination of his mother.

Val said, "Is that supposed to be funny?"

"If it is," said Emerson quietly, "it's in bad taste." He looked at Abby, noting her pallor, against which her mouth was shockingly red. He asked, "Abby?"

She was trying to recover herself, feeling the ground cut from under her feet, feeling herself sliding inexorably toward the edge of a precipice, toward an unimaginable destination. "Of course, it's a joke," she said.

Val looked sulky but relieved. She commented, "Barry has an odd sense of humor."

"Not at all," said Barry smoothly. "I didn't say that Abby had consented. I merely stated my intentions."

"Good boy," said Carstairs, "nothing like giving warning," and Val asked, setting down her glass, "Rushing your fences, aren't you, Barry?"

"There isn't much time," said Barry, "there never is." He looked at Emerson. "You aren't very talkative."

Emerson said, "No . . ." He rose. He said, "Sorry, Abby, but I must get back to work."

Barry spoke to Abby as if they were alone.

"Angry?" he inquired. "Madder'n hell?"

She said, "Yes . . ." but she smiled a little. Yet she was angry. He had no right, he was out of his mind. Carstairs was a stranger to her — she had met him only once. She had known Val for years, but Val was no intimate of hers. Craig was half brother, half potential lover, or had been. And Barry had made this outrageous statement to them all.

But the sensation of being in his arms was still strongly upon her, as if she had not left them. To look at him directly would be a betrayal.

He said, "You'll get over it."

Val rose. She said courteously, "It's been too fascinating. I have never seen anything like it away from the theater. Do let me know what happens in the next act. We'd better be going, Pete . . ." and as Abby rose she added, "Don't come. I'm sure you and Barry have so much to discuss. Why he wants to marry you and why you won't marry him." She was taut with fury but it was not in her husky voice or eyes. They were too cool. "I would suggest," she said, "the Good Will hour, or Town Hall —"

Abby was scarlet and helpless. Barry walked over to her and put his arm lightly around her shoulders. He said, "I couldn't enlist your special gifts on my side, could I, Val?"

Pete looked from one to the other. One for the book. He must repeat the conversation to Madge word for word. She would hate missing it.

A car drove up, a door slammed, there were voices and steps in the hall. Abby was white again, and Barry's arm tightened. She tried to move away. She heard Jay Morris's elderly, slow footsteps retreating toward the stairs, she heard her father's brisker tread, she heard him speak to a servant. "Where is Miss Abby?" he asked clearly.

He came through to the sun porch. Abby spoke to Barry just in time. She said low, savagely, "If you don't let me go I'll never forgive you," and Barry released her.

"Well," said Wallace pleasantly, "how gratifying. . . . Val, how are you? I haven't seen you in years. You are looking very well. Is there any tea, Abby? I quite forgot to have luncheon." He

84

looked at Carstairs and at Barry. His eyes remained on Barry, thoughtfully.

Abby made the presentations and wondered if he had heard her. Val was smiling at him. She said, "You should have been here a little earlier, Mr. Wallace."

He motioned toward the chairs they had left, "Please don't go," he said hospitably, "just as I come. Persuade your friends to stay," he told his daughter softly.

She was pouring his tea. Her hands shook perceptibly and Carstairs said, in pity for her, "Come along, Val, Madge expects us." He glanced at Barry but Barry shook his head, looking at Abby, the downbent head, the long hands busy with cool worn silver and cool porcelain.

Barry spoke to Abby, directly, again, as if they were alone. He asked, "Shall I stay, Abby?"

She felt the nervous tears in her throat, and against her eyelids. She said desperately, "No, Barry, please, not now."

In another moment they had gone, all of them. There was a long silence. The little maid, a local product, tiptoed in to light a lamp here and there, although it was unnecessary, and vanished. Wallace set down his cup.

He said, "The tea is cool and too strong. Where is Craig?"

"He was here, but he went back to the gallery."

"I see. And what was the meaning of that extraordinary little scene?" her father inquired.

She tried, as if by magic, to conjure up the sensation of Barry's arm around her, his nearness, his protective tenderness, and passion. It was of no use. She was alone, and afraid.

She said, "Nothing . . . just a – joke. You know Val."

"On the contrary," he said. "My knowledge of her is quite perfunctory. And this young man . . . Lambert . . . what am I to understand by this sudden intimacy between you? Because it is perfectly obvious."

She answered, "He came, about three. . . . Val and Mr. Carstairs rode over later."

"I am not interested in timetables," her father said. "What exactly happened here before I came in?"

She thought, Barry will be back . . . tonight, tomorrow. He will see Father. He will tell him . . . there's no use trying to evade it, now or any other time.

She said, "Barry asked me to marry him. He told . . . the others."

Wallace was very still. His face was gray and unrevealing. After a moment he said. "That's interesting. And are you going to marry him, Abby?"

Abby put her hands to her face, a frantic, childish gesture. She was more afraid than she had ever been, in all her life.

"Are you?" asked her father softly, insistently. "Are you?"

The tears ran between her fingers. She took her hands away and her face was devastated. She knew how he despised tears, how anything as purely physical as tears, a distorted mouth, or swollen eyes affected him. Long ago, when as a child she had cried bitterly because he had hurt her, he had said, "I am not moved by tears." He had looked at her with distaste and added, "You are very like your mother, in many ways."

She steadied her voice and answered. "I don't know, Father, *I don't know.*"

7

Wallace leaned back in his chair. His face was rigidly controlled, except his eyes. He said reflectively:

"A moment ago, I remarked that you are very like your mother. She was always" — he hesitated deliberately — "indecisive. It is a symptom of immaturity, and she was of course young . . . younger, when she died, than you are now."

Abby stared at him. Why was he talking to her of her mother? He rarely spoke of her. As a child, as a girl, Abby had begged him to . . . "Tell me about my mother . . . what was she like?" . . . but he had never done so. He had referred her to the portrait.

She asked, bewildered, "But what has that to do with —?"

He interrupted, lifting his hand in a mock apology. His smile was as taut as a tightrope. He spoke genially, as if he were amused by an entertaining memory. He said, "There was a brief time when she believed that she wished to leave me."

Abby felt strength flow back into her bones and blood. It was as if, for a split second, she could identify herself with a woman she had not known . . . a woman seeking escape, a girl, younger than herself, trying blindly to find release from a situation that had become intolerable. But why had he told her this? she thought. It was the one thing not in his character to admit. That is, if she knew him; and she thought she did. For he had an enormous, vulnerable pride.

She heard herself speak, quickly. "Why didn't she?" she demanded.

He smiled again, slyly. He spoke with relish, rolling the words on his tongue, savoring their implications.

"It took her some time," he said, "to make up her mind. And when she had done so, she found that she was pregnant." He looked at his daughter and his eyes glittered. "With you . . ." he added softly, unnecessarily.

He knew, as soon as he had spoken that he had made a serious error. Abby's face hardened, her mouth and eyes steadied. For a moment she forgot her own situation, forgot herself and Barry, thinking of a frightened girl.

She said hardily, "What difference would that make?"

"You're not very practical," said her father. "Look at it this way . . . what had she to return to? — A farmhouse," he said contemptuously, "cluttered with animal people . . . drudgery, reproaches."

"She would have had me."

"No. You," said her father, "are my child."

As simple as that. Nothing of her own, nothing with which to fight . . . no arms, no armor . . . against Wallace and his money, Wallace and his battery of lawyers.

It was as if he had read her mind. He said pleasantly, "She hadn't a chance."

"No," agreed Abby. "But I have."

Yes, a very grave error. He recognized it and shrank within himself, waiting to see how he could recover the lost ground. There was still a card he could play. He held it, waiting. . . .

She spoke first. "I wish I could have made it up to her."

"You read too much fiction," he told her. "What was there to make up, as you put it? Your mother had everything" — he hesitated again — "to live for," he concluded tritely, and watched her narrowly.

Something reached out and touched her with an icy finger but she shrugged it aside, too intent to trace it to its source. She said, "Barry and I are in love."

He said, "Love?" and laughed, not loudly. "Uniforms and medals."

"Barry isn't in uniform."

"He was," he reminded her, "a short time ago. It happens all the time — on dance floors or a park bench. Love is a romantic word. But not the right one. Sex," he suggested, "is as near as we can come to it without being — indelicate."

She asked low, "What's wrong with sex?"

"My dear child," he said, "it is hardly enough upon which to base a marriage."

Abby said, "No marriage would be much good without it!"

His had been. He had married a woman in order to add her to his collection . . . to give her her proper setting; to exhibit her when he wished and, when he did not wish, to keep her to himself. He had seemed marvelous to her, releasing her from monotony and hard work, from the eventual necessity of marrying some man like her father, with manure on his boots. So she had loved her husband with gratitude and an awkward ardor. There had been no one else to love.

He spoke evenly, and Abby was appalled. He said, "If that's what you want, it were better to sleep with — with this stranger, Abby, and get it out of your system."

She was very white. She cried, "You don't mean that!"

"In a way," he told her, "I do." But his control was briefly shattered, his face dark with revulsion. He said, recovering himself, "Once before I kept you from making a mistake."

"Malcolm?" she asked. "Not me. You persuaded him. He wanted me, but not without your money. He was very ambitious. You made it clear that by the time there was money for him to use, it would be too late."

He said smugly, "Of course. And he made an abrupt exit. He was a bright young man. An eighteen-year-old girl, without a sou to her name, would have been an emotional and financial drain. Yet, you were not grateful."

She said flatly, "I am, now. But not before. For most women, a bad marriage is better than none."

He said, "If you must marry . . ." and his slight emphasis on the word made her crawl all over as if she were suddenly unclean, "I would have no objection to your marrying Craig."

"I know," she said. "There have even been times when I considered it."

"You are going to tell me," he suggested, "that you could not – love him?"

Abby shook her head. "No, I have thought

92

that I could . . . that it would be easy, too easy," she said.

He was, she saw, a little startled. She was rarely able to startle him.

He said, "I am fond of Craig. I know him, and his background. You have had ample opportunity to know him, also. I would not have been unreasonable. . . ."

Not at all. He had planned it long ago. There was plenty of time. But eventually he would permit them to slip into marriage, and everything would go on much as it had, for years. The mixture as before. Abby would continue to decorate his house, to act as his secretary and hostess, her beauty maturing. He would of course speak privately to Craig . . . Dangerous, he would say, to consider the possibility of children. Her mother . . . she is very like her mother.

Abby said, "I suppose not. And we would have gone on living here. The only difference being that we would have had connecting rooms, Craig and I —"

"I see." He rose, a little stiffly. He said, "This has been a very unprofitable conversation."

Abby stood also. She said, "We haven't finished it."

"No?"

"But you have helped me make up my

mind. I'm going to tell Barry that I'll marry him."

He said, "You're of age, and there is nothing I can do except remind you that it will be without my approval or consent; that if you find, after all, that you have made a mistake, you need not look to me to help you remedy it." His hand tightened on the back of the chair from which he had risen. "And I must ask you not to see Mr. Lambert here . . . in my house."

She said, "His mother won't object to my going there, I think."

She walked past him. Her knees shook, but she could move . . . away from him, through the door. But he put out his hand and caught her by the wrist. His fingers were surprisingly strong. He drew her back until she faced him. He held her there. He had failed, once. He would try again.

He said:

"When I said I had no objection to your marrying Craig . . . it was not wholly true. But I have every reason to believe that he is devoted to you . . . and that the sacrifice which marriage to you would — or should — entail would not seem too great."

"Sacrifice?" she repeated uncomprehendingly. She tried to pull away but his fingers bit into the delicate flesh of her wrist. She said, frightened, "You're hurting me."

His fingers did not relax. He said, "I wish I need not, but you compel me." And she knew it was of physical hurt he spoke. "You are not stable emotionally, Abby," he went on. "It is an inherited instability. It caused your mother to destroy herself."

She was so white he thought she would fall. He released her, only to put his arm around her. He said, "Craig would have understood. I wonder if Mr. Lambert —" His voice trailed off. He added, "Because you must tell him, in simple justice. For men of Lambert's type — very masculine, very physical, expect their wives to bear children safely, if only as an extension of their own ego."

She whispered, her eyes strained and dilated, "Are you trying to tell me that my mother was *insane!*"

He said quickly:

"No. Insanity developing during pregnancy or following childbirth is precipitated, I believe, by those factors. It premises an unstable condition of the nervous system . . . which might never have manifested itself —" He shrugged, and released her. "Such a disturbance usually clears up, in time. As the doctors say, the prognosis is good . . . but further pregnancies would be a grave risk."

She asked, still whispering, "I could *inherit* this . . . ?"

"I don't know, Abby. The predisposition, possibly."

Abby cried, "I don't believe you. You are trying to frighten me, you are trying to prevent my marriage to Barry."

"Of course," he said, "what else?"

"Who was my mother's doctor?" she demanded.

"His name," said Wallace, "was Gilpin . . . a very famous obstetrician, in New York. He came here, at my request, with his staff." He added, "He died some years ago."

She said dully, "I don't want to hear any more."

He watched her move, walk away, his face composed, and his eyes intent.

Somehow she managed to get upstairs. She did not hear Craig come out into the hall, she did not hear him speak her name. He watched her, frowning, and then went out into the sun porch. Wallace was still there. Craig asked, more abruptly than usual, "What's the matter with Abby?"

Wallace said, "Find the bell and ring, will you? I'd like some sherry."

"She looked dreadful," said Craig, obeying.

"Abby? She's very emotional," said her father.

"And my opposition to young Lambert. . . ."

Craig asked quickly, "She actually intends to marry him?"

Wallace sighed. "Perhaps," he said. "I don't know. Yet I think I have persuaded her that it would be a very reckless error."

Craig sat down, and took his cigarette case from his pocket. He said, "It's been something of a blow to me, too."

"I know," said Wallace, "but if you will take advice hard for young people to accept, then I counsel patience."

Their eyes met for an instant. Craig shivered, and looked away. They understood each other. He thought, What has he said, or done? She wouldn't look like that merely because he had said he didn't approve. She's of age, she can marry whom she pleases.

He was far from being stupid. He knew where his interests lay, he was aware of his obligations. He wanted to run quickly up the stairs, to take Abby's hands in his, to cry, What has he done to you, tell me, perhaps I can help!

He knew what that would mean, too. He consoled himself by thinking, as a little later he accepted the glass of sherry from Wallace's hands, that there was nothing he could do. He possessed a natural caution, it was difficult to override it. Besides, had not Wallace counseled patience?

In her room, grown suddenly unfamiliar, the walls diminished to the proportions of a cell, Abby sat huddled in a chair. Her forehead was wet and her hands. Her hands were very cold, but her head burned and ached under the suddenly unendurable weight of her hair. What shall I do? she thought.

She thought further, starkly, My mother went insane after I was born and killed herself.

There were doctors she could consult, books she could read. No, a simpler way — Why should she have a child? She thought, We wouldn't need a child, we would have each other. She had never cared for children, especially. She had known few, and those briefly. They intimidated her, with their wisdom, their innocence and cruelty. But she knew nothing of Barry's views on the matter.

She knew nothing of Barry, except that he had said he loved her. It was the one important thing, the only thing that mattered.

If a man and woman loved each other, surely it was enough, they need have no more. Children did not always form a bond, she argued, they sometimes created a barrier. She had no wish to share or to be shared. She wanted Barry;

he was complete, in himself, as she would be complete, with him.

How long she sat there she did not know. She thought, but, if I tell him . . . ?

After a long time someone knocked at the door. She said, "Come in," indifferently and looked up to see Craig standing there. He asked carefully, "Abby, are you ill?"

"No."

He sat down on the edge of the bed. He said, "Uncle Norman suggested that you might like a tray, up here."

"All right," she said, with an effort.

"Abby, for heaven's sake. . . ."

She said, "Craig, go away . . . there's nothing you can do."

He said incredulously, "I can't believe it . . . A man you never saw until — was it yesterday? It's out of all reason."

"I suppose so," she said.

He leaned forward. "Abby . . . Uncle Norman asked me what, exactly, had taken place before he came in this afternoon. I was there, I saw, and heard . . . I told him. He seemed relieved."

She looked at him for the first time. The color came back slowly to her lips and cheeks. She asked, "Why?"

Craig looked away. He found himself extremely embarrassed.

"He didn't take the − proposal at its face value," he answered.

Abby stiffened. She said, "I see. . . ."

Craig rose. He said, "I'm sorry you're angry at me. But thinking it over, Abby, there wasn't much to say." He stopped, and then added casually, "Uncle Norman had a further suggestion . . . that you might want to go away for a time."

"With whom?" she inquired.

"With him," he said, "and me. Somewhere amusing, perhaps. . . ."

She asked stonily, "To spare me the embarrassment of running after a man who had announced his public intention of marrying me in the spirit of good clean fun?"

He said uneasily, "That's not exactly how he put it."

Abby rose. She asked, "That's how you'd put it, Craig?"

"Oh, come," said Craig, "the man's obviously crazy about you, Abby, but −"

She said, after a moment, "Ask Mrs. Gambel if she can send the tray up early, will you?"

"All right," he said. The door closed after him, and she stood there, shaking with anger. Her father believed . . . Craig believed. . . .

They were wrong. They would soon know, she thought, how wrong they were. Anger was a tonic. It was wonderful, it informed her, revitalizing. It was a good clean flame. . . .

Abby's tray had been sent upstairs. A little later it reposed on a table in the wide hall from which her room opened, the plates almost untouched. Her door was shut, and locked.

Abby sat down at her desk, picked up the telephone and dialed a number. She had had to look the number up in the directory. She remembered that then her hands shook, her eyes blurred. But her hands were steady now and she spoke quietly into the receiver.

"This is Miss Wallace," she said, "may I speak with Mr. Lambert?"

He came so instantly, he must have been close to the telephone. His voice was warm and eager, as urgent as if it spoke to her from the room in which she sat.

"Abby, for God's sake . . . I was just going to call you."

She asked, "Could you come here, Barry? Tonight?"

"Right away," he said. He did not say goodbye. She heard him replace the instrument, with a miniature crash. The line buzzed like an angry wasp.

Abby went to her clothes closet, and opened the door. Her own things hung there, the tweed skirts, a few cotton and linen frocks. They had been of her choosing. The others she had hated always because they were right only for her or a woman long dead. They were not the sort of clothes you could lend to another girl, to a friend – if you had one – and say, "Here, wear this, you're about my size." Even Val, who was a model, couldn't wear these.

She took one from the padded, scented hanger. She disliked it, as she disliked everything her father preferred, as she disliked the effeminate brilliant designer who had made it. But tonight it would serve her.

It was a white, straight-falling dress, fashioned from a fine heavy crepe, almost unobtainable now. The high girdle was woven of gold and silver thread, and the round neck and long wide sleeves were intricately embroidered. It was a lovely dress, a picture dress, and a little strange.

Abby loosened her hair, and parted it. It sprang upward from the parting, strong, curling. She brushed it over her ears, and coiled it low at her neck. . . .

Silver-gilt slippers . . . the sheerest stockings she owned . . . the brief undergarments. No girdle. She had never worn one.

Powder, lipstick . . . the stopper of a perfume bottle drawn across the palms of her hands, at the base of her throat. She leaned close to the mirror, the pupils of her eyes dilated and black.

Someone plodded to the door and reported, knocking, "Mr. Lambert to see you, Miss Wallace."

Abby said clearly, "I'll be right down."

She didn't move. She sat still by the mirror looking at the familiar face. She saw it one way; and he, another. How? And for how long? Could heavy gold hair and an especial modeling of bone and flesh hold a man forever, for as long as he lived? No. No face, not even that of Helen. But something else could hold him . . . and that was love, passionate, singlehearted. If a man had that, if he knew it; if it was as certain as sunrise, as dependable as the bread he earned and ate, would he look farther afield?

She left the room and went downstairs. She did not see her father, with Craig beside him, emerge from the library and look up at her. She did not see her father's hand close on the younger man's arm and the door of the room they had just left shut behind them again.

Each remembered her, as she had looked at that moment, for a long time, after his own fashion . . . Abby, wearing white with silver and gold embroidery . . . walking slowly down the curving stairs as if in her dreaming sleep, seeing nothing, yet with her eyes wide open.

8

Barry had been shown into the small morning room. When she came to the door he was standing, with his back to her, looking at the portrait of her mother. He was incongruous in that setting, the delicate gilts and pastels, the faded brocade, the inlaid secretary, the heavy silk draperies, drained rose. He dwarfed it, he made the décor generally appear trivial, too fragile, a little mannered, even silly. He was such a big young man.

He turned and saw her. He asked, "Isn't there anywhere else?" He smiled with his mouth but his eyes were grave. "This seems somewhat public."

Everything was public, in this house, which had so many rooms and so few people.

He said, staring, "You look . . . you look . . . I don't believe it. I can't." He raised a shoulder toward the portrait. "That was your mother?"

"Yes."

"It frightened me at first," he said, "she doesn't look quite of this world."

Abby said, not looking at the portrait, "I know."

It was a curious conversation. He had not taken her hands nor spoken her name.

"You are," he said, "of course. Abby, get a wrap or something. It isn't cold, but you might need it. We'll take the car and get out of this."

He walked beside her, not touching her, into the hall. There was a concealed closet there, set in the paneling. She opened it and took the first coat she put her hand on . . . it had no alliance with her frock nor her little slippers nor her heavy shining hair. It was a light, sturdy tweed, which smelled faintly of wood smoke and tobacco. It belonged to Craig.

She threw it around her shoulders and went out into the warm darkness of the May night and without a word got into the car. Barry engaged the gears and drove off down the driveway, fast, as if they were pursued. He said, without looking at her,

"Did you have a pretty rugged time after I left?"

"In a way."

"I should have stayed. I'm a damned fool. But I thought you wanted me to go."

"Barry, I did."

"I shouldn't give in to you. What sort of man is your father? I've never seen anyone like him before."

She said, "It would take me a lifetime to tell you, I think."

"You'll have it," he promised. They left the grounds and he turned and drove rapidly along the main road, turned again, and entered a winding, irregular road that rose to a ridge, overlooking the foothills. There were a few scattered houses here and some wide, sloping fields. He pulled off into one of them, and stopped the car. He spoke her name, harshly.

"Abby?"

He took her in his arms and kissed her. She could feel him shaking, she heard his voice saying crazy, wonderful things, over and over, and his voice, too, was out of control. A deep, penetrating delight rose within her, it was as if detached, outside herself. It had nothing to do with the satisfaction of his kiss, the warmth and strength of his body, the instant, almost painful response of her own. It was part of these, but it was beyond them. It had to do only with herself. It had to do with a knowledge more marvelous than the acceleration of pulse, the fever in the blood.

She told herself, *He belongs to me.*

It was an almost savage awareness, as if she

had been born blind and, in darkness, dreamed of light, imagining it, feeling the warmth of the sun but never seeing it, but knowing always that the sun was there. Now, she saw.

Barry belonged to her; and because he belonged, she could immerse herself in him, she could be one with him, beyond the body's union.

She found that she was crying, almost without tears, hard, harsh sobbing, sudden and uncontrollable.

Barry held her close. He said, frightened, "Abby, for God's sake . . . darling, what is it?"

He had heard wounded men cry like that . . . going on for a moment after they were hit, or falling, immediately, and silent, and then, suddenly, the rending sound that had not much to do with pain as with shock.

Abby made a desperate effort. She fought the sobbing, and whimpered, a little, like a child. She said hoarsely, unsteadily, "I'm sorry, but I'm so happy."

"*You're* happy?" he said, his hands on her hair. It was satin to the touch. He wondered that it did not burn with a pale flame, one which you could feel but which did not hurt you.

She said, "Now, I can love."

It was a curious thing to say. He did not remember it, until long afterward; that is, he did not turn it over in his mind, examining and weighing it.

He said, "Look . . . we must do a little planning as it's perfectly obvious that your father hates my guts."

Abby said, "He wouldn't express it quite that way. But he doesn't know you and," she added, "he says I don't."

"Nuts to that," said Barry cheerfully. "What else has he against me?"

She said, "I don't know."

But her heart hammered and she thought, I must tell him . . . now.

She did not. She heard him say:

"It can't be money. I've my salary and a supplementary income from my father's estate. There's also my mother's, but I hope she lives to be a hundred. By then she will have spent anything not legally nailed down. It's okay by me. Abby, will you mind living in my apartment? You've heard Mother describe it. It's not that bad, of course. We might not be able to find another place in the district and I want to stay there. I'm getting tangled up in politics to some extent. I can vote, in November, as I've had New York residence for years . . . But, it isn't much of a flat. Would you mind?"

"Of course not," she said.

She had heard nothing, except would she mind if she lived where he lived. Absurd question. She was not concerned with money or politics or with his interests outside herself . . . her concern lay only in what was happening, now, and what would further happen, to them mutually.

He said, "We can drive somewhere tomorrow, have the medical tests and get the license. It's a five-day wait — I looked it up after I left you this afternoon. You have to be married in the town in which the license was procured. We'll pick one that hasn't a newspaper."

She said, "All right."

He took her by the shoulders and shook her, slightly, "You sound as if you were talking in your sleep," he complained. "Take a little interest, will you? We're planning an elopement." He stopped. "Or would you rather be married at home or in church, all that sort of thing?" he asked gently.

She said, "No."

"If you're thinking," he said, "that your father would raise hell, we could be married from Mother's place."

She turned and clung to him.

"No," she said. "No! Just us . . . no one else, Barry, no one we know."

He was astonished and disturbed by her vehemence. He thought, I don't blame her, she's been kicked around long enough . . . and even if that old so-and-so broke down and gave in, it would be only to save his face.

"Me too," he said. "There's been enough public marrying in my family to last a couple of generations." He laughed and held her hard against him. "So I'll look at the road map and take Mother's coupons and we'll drive up tomorrow. I'll pick you up at the end of your drive . . . say ten o'clock. What a story to tell our kids . . . Mom and Pop met, fell in love at first sight, took a second look and got married. Then we'll say, 'If you follow our example we'll beat the hell out of you.' Abby, what's the matter?"

She said faintly, "I forgot —"

"Forgot what? You're shivering . . . darling, are you cold?"

She said, "No . . . wait a minute, Barry, let me go." She sat away from him, not touching him. She asked, "Barry, do you want children?"

"Well, sure," he said, astonished, "half a dozen . . . out of the lot we should get one as beautiful as you and one as smart as I."

He was laughing but when he heard her voice again he was silent. She said painfully, "My father told me today that after my birth my mother went insane and killed herself."

He felt the shock, like bitterly cold water. He

said, after a minute, "And you didn't know, until this afternoon?"

"No."

"My God," he said, "you poor kid." His arm was around her instantly, he was drawing her close again, and she submitted. She did not cry now . . . which was strange, he thought, afterward. She leaned against him, waiting.

He said, "You can't let that frighten you, darling. It doesn't mean that you — "

"How do I know?" she asked passionately. "If this makes any difference to you, Barry — "

She was praying, in her heart. She was saying, Let it not make any difference, please, please.

He said, "Why should it? Don't be a little fool. He was probably trying to frighten you. Yes, that's it. Otherwise, why wouldn't he have told you long before this? After we're married we can talk to doctors about it, get their opinion, if it would make you feel any better. And, anyway, it's matrimony that we're rushing into, not parenthood. You're just a kid," he said, "there's plenty of time."

He had been shocked but he had rallied. Old woman's tales. The hell with it. And any woman who had been married to Norman Wallace, he reflected, doubtless had every reason to go crazy, baby or no baby.

He said that to Abby, a little differently. He said, "You're marrying me!"

It was all right, everything was all right. She drew a long shaken breath.

"Yes," she said, "I'm marrying you."

He kissed her then, and was as triumphantly astonished by her response as he had been earlier. Releasing her, he said, "Well, you never know —"

"What?" she asked unsteadily.

"The contents from the package. The wrappings differ ... pretty, attractive, exciting, beautiful — in your case, all of them — but whether the contents are cold or —"

"Barry!"

"Okay," he said, laughing. He thought of Val. Her wrapping was exciting enough and all but labeled dynamite. But, was she? Sometimes he had believed, yes; but more often, no. For a very brief moment he was disconcerted to realize that now he would never find out.

He asked, "Darling, how much will you hate me, if I tell you I'm hungry?"

"Hungry?" said Abby. She thought a moment and then said, with amazement, "So am I. Starving."

"Did you have dinner?" he asked.

"On a tray. I didn't eat it."

"I didn't even have a tray," he said. "Mother's

meals are movable feasts. You phoned at the cocktail hour, so to speak. I departed at once."

"Without dinner?"

"Without dinner; without, I may add, cocktails. There's a species of log roadhouse not far from here. I wouldn't advise the village, we might run into someone we know. Let's go, shall we?"

The roadhouse was built of logs, it had a neon sign, and looked a little sinister, which it was not. It was hardly more than a glorified diner. They were alone in it, except for the counterman, the short-order cook, the man at the bar, and a couple of customer truck drivers. Barry and Abby sat at a rough table under a low ceiling festooned with artificial leaves and ate fried-egg sandwiches, and drank coffee.

"I for one," said Barry, "need no intoxicants. . . . Have you any idea how beautiful you are?"

She had accepted the fact that she was beautiful, from the time when she grew up and fell in love with Malcolm; when she no longer had braces on her teeth, nor needed glasses; when her father first looked at and saw her. She had accepted it as she accepted any fact, as she had accepted the beauty glowing on the walls of the gallery, the flesh tones of a Rubens, the pink-washed loveliness of a Corot.

But it had meant nothing to her, until earlier this evening when she had taken the white dress from the hanger, when she had looked in the mirror. Then, for the first time, it had reassured her, it had been her friend. Now it was more than her friend. It was a weapon . . . that and her love . . . these were all she would ever need.

They ate, with hunger; and with hunger, looked at one another. The counterman watched them, and spoke to the man at the bar. "Wallace's daughter," said one. "Boy, is she a knockout!" and the other asked, "Ain't that guy young Lambert? There was a piece in the paper I seen . . . and a picture . . . looks tough, don't he?"

They watched them go out, the tweed coat over Abby's arm, the white dress subtly molded to her body, the wonderful hair.

Driving back, she asked, suddenly remembering, "Barry, what will your mother say?"

"She'll cry," he replied promptly; "she'll come all over romantic, and give you a string of pearls. The second best. She'll love it, Abby. She adores elopements."

"But me?" asked Abby.

"She likes you," said Barry, "and if she didn't, she'd be unperturbed, I think. When I was a kid and she gave me a gadget which I'd promptly break, she'd tell me I was stupid or clumsy or a dope generally. Then she'd replace it. I'm afraid she thinks of marriage in that way. She's always been able to replace hers."

"I see," said Abby. "And do you feel that way too?"

"I should," he answered, "if the psychologists are right. But I don't seem to fit into a case history book. Didn't I tell you I had no inhibitions? I should be insecure and unhappy, if only subconsciously, because I've survived not only one broken home but several. But it didn't work out that way. As for our marriage, we aren't dealing in generalities, are we? It's you and me, as I see it. For good."

She said, "That's the way you want it?"

"How else?" he asked, half angrily. "Look, we've a lifetime ahead in which to argue and analyze. Is that enough for you?"

It was more than enough. It was everything. Everything?

They had turned into her driveway when she touched his arm. She said, "Maybe I've accepted reassurance too easily. I've been very selfish. You were – kind, you said all the right things, but you should have time in which to think it over."

"Think what over? Have you lost your mind?" he asked reasonably.

"Just that," she said haltingly, "that I *might*. . ."

"I wish it were feasible," he said, "to turn you over my knee and whale the daylights out of you. I thought we'd settled that. We'll consult the whole medical directory, if it will make you any happier. But after we are married, not before. And we'll begin with your mother's doctor . . . as I assume she had one."

"He's dead," she said. "I asked."

"So what? There are always ouija boards."

"Don't joke."

"Who's joking?" he asked. "You're as stubborn as I am, Abby. There must be records. We'll track them down."

"And if it was true . . . what my father said . . . and if the doctors told you that I shouldn't have children?"

"Then we won't have 'em."

He stopped the car. He asked, "Shall I come in with you?"

"I'd rather not."

"Frightened?"

She bent to kiss him, fleetly. She said, "I'll never be, again."

"Tomorrow," he said, "at ten."

"I'll be scared?" she inquired and laughed.

"You ought to be," he said, "it's customary."

He waited in the car until she had gone in,

and then turned and drove away. Tomorrow was a long way off, and five days from tomorrow was an eternity. He thought of her in his arms; he thought of the feel of her hair under his hands, of the texture of her skin; the warmth of her mouth. He thought of her gravity and her laughter, her silences and her speech. He thought of her eyes and their heavy white lids . . . he thought of the life they would have together.

He thought of what she had told him, and dismissed it until it became necessary to think of it again. Either Wallace had lied or he had not. If he had lied, that was that; if he hadn't there were good doctors still available, better perhaps than twenty-odd years ago. Whatever they decided. . . .

He was unused to tenderness, and now was shaken by it. He could not express it with any accuracy. He thought merely, Poor kid. . . .

Abby moved quietly through the big hall. Remembering Craig's coat she took it from her shoulders and put it on a chair. She looked at the library door but it did not open. She went alone, unquestioned, up the stairs and to her room.

Craig had gone to bed. Wallace, in the library, had heard the car drive up. He had gone to the windows and looked out, and seen them there in the light from the doorway. He had watched them, forcing himself. And had gone through the library into the anteroom from which a door led into the corridor to the gallery. He had found Morris there but had not spoken to him. Instead, he had shut himself in one of the rooms, sitting there, looking with concentration at the pictures. They were his. They were hung upon the walls. They would remain there until he died; after which he would not care what became of them.

9

Abby and Barry drove north through the misty
May morning to a border village. Sleepy and incurious, it lay in a cup of the round hills, which
flowed, faintly green, into the mountains . . .
and steeples pointed their white fingers toward
a tender blue sky.

She was frightened . . . ice slithered along her
spine, her scalp prickled, her knees were fluid
and her lips bone-dry. . . . But not all the time,
not for long. When they walked into the square-
towered Town Hall, Barry kept her hand close
in his, his vitality flowed into her, it was
warmth and reassurance. The clerk was old and
dusty, his questions were like bird shot rattling
around them. But he, too, was incurious, overworked, as was the physician, intercepted just
as he was leaving his house to make a call.

Driving back, Barry said, "Scared again,
weren't you? Yet you promised, you wouldn't
be . . . ever."

She tried to laugh, looking at him, the big, self-assured young man. She said, "But, Barry, it's natural," in apology, touching his hand as it lay, relaxed, upon the wheel.

He said, "You can still get out of it. Today isn't irrevocable. There are five days left."

"Five hundred years." Her voice shook. "I wish I could sleep tonight and wake on the fifth day."

"If you feel like that . . . everything will be all right. Abby, you haven't said anything about a honeymoon. You haven't said anything," he repeated, "about a ring, for instance. A girl's entitled to a ring . . . I think — emeralds or rubies. . . . Diamonds are too hard, too bright."

She said, "Who wants rings? And I thought . . . that is, I assumed, we were just going to your apartment."

"Never assume. I did considerable telephoning last night. We are going to Hot Springs. It's pretty there, this time of year . . . perhaps you already know that? I've wangled a couple of weeks off. God knows," he added with some rancor, "it wasn't hard, I'll never be missed." He laughed. He said, "I walked to the village to telephone from a booth — and roused up an old friend and put him on to getting hotel and train reservations . . . I felt like a conspirator, letting myself in the house at all hours. Mother came paddling to the stairway. She said, 'Where on earth have you been?' and didn't wait for an answer. It seems that Val – " He broke off. "You aren't listening!" he accused her.

"Just to your voice," she admitted drowsily. She was sleepy, suddenly; empty, yet filled with sleep. It was a curious sensation.

"Did you have breakfast?" he demanded.

"Coffee."

"That all? You must be starved. This has all taken time. You're a crazy little thing," he said roughly, "you have no sense at all."

She said, "I tried to eat."

The dining room, and the early sun, and her father appearing unexpectedly. He never appeared at breakfast – why today? Sitting there remote and withdrawn, looking at her now and then. Craig, yawning a little, looking apprehensive. Her toast crumbled on her plate, her orange juice untouched, the smell of eggs making her sick.

"Okay," Barry said, "so you tried. Next town we come to, we'll stop for lunch. Come closer. I'm an excellent one-arm driver. I've had," he said proudly, "practice."

"Don't tell me about it," said Abby.

"Why not? No details, no chapter and verse . . . ?"

"Sometime," she said, "not now." She

thought, Sometime when I am sure, after we are married. Sometime. Then I can ask him . . . Who was the first girl you fell in love with, who were the others . . . what did they look like, what did they mean to you? When did you know that this one or that was not the one you really wanted? Sometime I can ask . . . What were you like when you were eight and when you were twelve . . . what excited you, what depressed you? Tell me about your schools and the boys you knew . . . tell me about what happened to you in camp here . . . and in Italy . . .

The next town had a frame hotel, with verandas on the street and across the second story. It was late, they were alone in the dining room except for a gaunt waitress, her gray hair incongruously caught in a fuchsia-colored snood. The soup was cold, the lamb was aged mutton, the mashed potatoes sodden lumps; the coffee couldn't have been worse and the pie had soaked through its shiny, tasteless crust.

Barry said, "It's a legend, you know."

"What is?"

"That all New England cooking is good."

She said, smiling a little. "Mine's good, *and* New England."

He said, "It's almost too much for any man to ask . . . a girl who looks like you and can cook.

Shall I ever tire of looking at you? Wasn't there a poem something like that? . . . Your hair," he said, "it lights up this room, like a beacon."

"But doesn't," she suggested, "warm the potatoes."

"Who cares? Eat something. Anything. The bread's not bad," he told her, "nor the soda crackers. And the pickles are very good. Abby, this is going to be wonderful. How uninteresting to marry a girl you have known all your life or with whom you have shared a long engagement, or even one you have known six weeks, a month, a week . . . nothing new to learn . . . or," he said, smiling, "not much . . . except, of course, the less agreeable discoveries they tell us we all make, after marriage, whether the foreknowledge has been long or short."

She said gravely, "I shall never discover — the disagreeable."

"Don't say it," he said; "you begin to frighten me. But take this hypothetical girl — by now I'd know her handicap at golf, her ping-pong record, her taste in clothes, perfume, theater, books, music . . . and if she were allergic to poison ivy, mother-in-law, shrimp, or preferred Scotch to bourbon . . . whether mysteries kept her awake nights — or if she put herself to sleep with essays and biographies. I know nothing about you, Abby, really. You hold endless possibilities. You can swim," he said, smiling, "but what else . . . ride? shoot? fish?"

She said, "I ride . . . I play golf, passably. I don't like tennis, much. No, I don't shoot . . . and I've not been fishing since I was a child."

"Well," he said, "I can see where I'll have to start you, from scratch . . . on a liberal education. Very liberal."

She said, her heart lifting, "I can at least take you on a tour of art galleries. I'm good, really . . . it should be most educational."

"Wonderful," said Barry. "And when they ask me, What's your wife like? and I say, Oh, utterly *un*like, I assure you, but she knows her way around art galleries – " He broke off. "Abby, I can't believe it," he said.

"I can't either."

No, she could not. It was like living in another world, it was like looking through a door into still another, new-minted, strange, disturbingly beautiful.

Barry overtipped the waitress, who wafted into the kitchen and informed a moody, incredulous cook that a couple of movie stars had stopped in for lunch. No, she didn't know who they was, but she was sure to God she'd seen 'em sometime or other. . . .

They drove on and reached, after too short a time, the entrance gates of the Wallace house.

Here they parted, having made their plans. Abby walked up the driveway, in her plain little shirtwaist frock, her bright head uncovered, her small, scuffed shoes light on the gravel. What she had to do was not too difficult. She had five days in which to pack her things, to be sent on later; to pack a suitcase with immediate needs. . . . "For God's sake, don't stagger out to meet me with eighteen pieces of luggage; there are shops at the hotel; you can buy what you need there to tide you over," he had said.

In five days, with the suitcase ready, she would wait at the driveway. Mrs. Gambel would help her. She was a dour, reliable woman. They had always liked each other.

When she reached the big hall it seemed very cold, and seemed dark. She blinked against the darkness, her eyes accommodating themselves slowly. She had reached the stairs when her father materialized, gray, from the gray light. She had not heard him, and her nerves shivered.

He asked, staring at her, "Where have you been?"

Abby steadied her breath. She said, for doubtless he knew as much, "With Barry."

"As I thought. There were guests for luncheon. Your friend Miss Stanley telephoned. She asked if you were here. When I said no, she inquired if Mr. Lambert had been." He added, with some satisfaction, "I took the call."

Abby said, "I had forgotten there were to be luncheon guests."

"Naturally," said her father, "in your present state." He added, "I have put Craig to work on the problem of our reservations."

"Reservations?" she repeated blankly.

Wallace said impatiently, "Really, Abby, you are impossible. Craig told you that I was planning a trip. I think a change would be quite beneficial for us all, at this point," he added.

She asked carefully, "Where are we going . . . and when?"

Wallace shrugged. He said, "Traveling is uncertain at best — one cannot leave at a moment's notice. But I have selected Pinehurst, and I hope we can leave in, approximately, a week's time."

He was watching her, closely. Resentment or astonishment or both were expected of her. She tried to register and convey these convincingly. She said, "But when Craig spoke to me about it I didn't say I'd go."

"You have no choice," said Wallace smoothly. "I am giving the staff a holiday as we shall be gone six weeks. Jay remains behind to work on the catalogue but a local woman will come in daily to clean and cook for him. Except for her — "

Abby was not listening. Six weeks? She thought. I'll be gone too, and forever – into that other world of which you have no knowledge.

He said, very sharply, "Must you stand there like an imbecile?" The word bit into her, shook her back into the present, the immediate. "How can you so cheapen yourself, Abby? If you are not humiliated, I am, for you . . . sneaking out of your house to meet, to pursue this man."

She said, "You said you would not have him here."

"From now on," he said, unmoving, "I advise that you remain at home, and get your personal belongings in readiness for the trip."

It was, she thought, fortuitous, and the perfect excuse. She could have trunks brought down, pack and label them, and leave them in Mrs. Gambel's care.

"All right," she said, and went on up the stairs. Wallace stood at the foot, looking up, frowning, after her.

In her room, her elation left her. She sat down on the edge of the bed, trembling. She thought, All today, when I was with Barry, we did not speak of my mother.

Was it possible that either had forgotten? All day, driving up to the little town, driving back, she had not once thought . . . and he had not spoken.

She rose and went to the interphone and spoke into it. She asked, "Is Mrs. Gambel there?" and when Mrs. Gambel came and her matter-of-fact voice answered, wheezily, Abby asked, "Would you come up, Mrs. Gambel, I want to talk to you about packing."

Something clicked, faintly . . . anyone could listen over the interphone.

She waited for Mrs. Gambel, wondering how much to tell, or if it was too soon to tell anything. Perhaps this woman who had been with the Wallaces since Abby's childhood was not, after all, attached to her. Why should she be? Perhaps, as was proper, her loyalty would be to her employer.

But in the long ago, when a governess was unkind, when a childish plan went wrong, when something happened to upset her, it was always to Mrs. Gambel that she had gone, sitting in the housekeeper's close, cluttered little living room, drinking the cambric tea she made her, listening to the stories of a Vermont village of another era.

Mrs. Gambel knocked.

"Come in," said Abby, her eyes wide, and the color draining from her face.

Mrs. Gambel came in. She was an almost

square woman, with thin gray hair combed upward and pinned in a hard, tight knot. She was conscious of her position. She wore decent black, and rarely an apron. She ran the house with ease and efficiency, even with her present diminished staff.

"What's wrong?" she asked instantly.

Someone had to help. There was no one but this woman. No one she trusted, as much. Yet she did not wholly trust her.

Abby said, "I want you to help me. . . ."

Mrs. Gambel stood, uncompromising. She asked, cautiously, "How?"

"Sit down," said Abby, making up her mind. And when Mrs. Gambel was sitting, very erect on the edge of the chair, she told her, and waited.

"It shouldn't be hard," said Mrs. Gambel slowly, with a gleam in her brown eyes.

Abby relaxed; relief was almost as sickening as tension. She said, "There's only you, Mrs. Gambel."

"I know," said Mrs. Gambel. She added, "You pack your things. I'll take what you want to have pressed and see that it's done. I'll carry your suitcase to the entrance myself." She added briskly, "You'll leave me the address for the trunks?"

Abby said, in wonder, "Is it as easy as that?"

She looked at the older woman. "If my father finds out that you helped me, you'll be discharged," she warned her.

"And without a character," said Mrs. Gambel grimly. "But I've money saved, and my house, at home. In another two years I was leaving anyway. As for my character, that's my own and no one can take it away from me. I wouldn't have stayed on this long if it hadn't been for the little I could do for you. Little enough."

She rose. She said, "Don't worry, Miss Abby. He won't find out. Even if he does, a good housekeeper isn't easy to find these days. He's used to having things run just so, his way. He'd not like breaking someone else in."

She smiled, turning at the door. She said, "I got a look at the young man the other afternoon. I liked what I saw of him. I hope you'll be happy. Marriage isn't easy, not even when you bring the best will in the world to it, Miss Abby. It's give-and-take and there's usually one who does most of the taking. Darius Gambel was of that mind," she said reminiscently, "but I managed him . . . and if he hadn't died, we'd be together yet."

The door closed after her but a moment later Abby opened it softly. She had heard her father's voice on the landing. It was low, but it carried. He was saying pleasantly, "Miss Abby sent for you, Mrs. Gambel?"

Mrs. Gambel explained sedately, "About the trunks. . . . I'm afraid that Nellie isn't very expert as yet. She hasn't had the experience. But she can do the necessary pressing, and I'll help with the actual packing," she added, "Miss Abby needn't worry. . . ."

She raised her voice a little; and it, too, carried.

"Very well," said Wallace, "naturally we count on you, in any emergency."

She said severely, "Certainly, Mr. Wallace."

10

"It seems funny," remarked Abby, "not to have a trousseau. . . ."

"Engagement, trousseau," said Barry tolerantly, "so what? They come later. You are looking very beautiful, Mrs. Lambert."

They were driving back to Fairton, after their marriage. The salt-box parsonage had been quiet, the sun coming in at the windows. A fly had buzzed persistently and the clergyman's voice had been old and a little shaky. His wife and a sentimental spinster daughter were the witnesses. The daughter had gone out to her garden and picked a handful of flowers, bleeding heart, mertensia, scrambled into a prim little bouquet, and thrust it in Abby's hands. She still held it, the flowers wilting.

She wore a dark silk suit and her hat was a twist of silk, haloing her head. She was very pale but her lips were bravely red, and her eyes burned bright. On her left hand she wore her wedding ring, and the square emerald that flanked it.

She turned her hand and the emerald caught the sun and threw it back again in darts of purest green.

He said, "I employed my five days well . . . I'm glad you like the ring."

Emerald or glass, it made no difference; he had given it to her. She smiled at him and he added, "As for the apartment, looking at it through your absent eyes, the less said the better. But Mother will be enchanted to haul some furniture from the attic and do something about things."

"What things?"

"Women-things," he said vaguely, "slip covers, curtains. Oh, hell, who cares?" He added, "We were nearly late to our wedding. I could strangle Val. It seemed almost deliberate malice on her part . . . yet it couldn't have been. I got out so quietly . . . and so early, after coffee in the kitchen. And there she was, about to take a prebreakfast dip in the pool. For the first time in her life, I bet. She was solicitous *and* curious. Ten to one, as soon as the car drove out she was upstairs hammering at Mother's door and announcing that I was off on some nefarious errand."

"I thought she was going back to town."

"The weekend has extended itself," said Barry.

"I wish she had," said Abby.

He grinned, "You don't like her much, darling, do you?"

"I'm a little afraid of her," said Abby. "Even as a child she was always so — I don't know how to put it — scornful, I suppose. Coming up to play with me, as if it were a condescension."

"Princess in rags," said Barry. "Daresay it was her type of compensation for the things you had and she had not. She is, however," he remarked, "a slick chick. Vining would have gone for her. . . ."

He seemed, suddenly, quite far away, and Abby asked, "Who's Vining?"

"A guy I used to know," said Barry shortly, "a very good guy." He was silent, remembering.

Abby touched his sleeve.

"Come back to me," she said softly.

He shrugged. "Vining's dead," he told her; "and because he's dead I'm alive. Let's not talk about him today . . . I've been thinking of him a lot recently. I suppose . . . false rumors of invasion, all that sort thing." He looked away and his hands were restless on the wheel. He said, "Sometimes I ask myself what the hell I'm doing here. Oh, don't argue, I know . . . but I still *ask*."

His mood was strange to her; she was silent, adjusting herself. And presently he inquired, "Not sorry that we phoned home, are you?"

"No." She wasn't, now. Now she felt secure. But she hadn't wanted Barry to telephone. Couldn't they just be married, just go away? But he had said, no, they couldn't. It was kinder to prepare Madge.

"You never know," he'd said, "when she'll go to pieces or stay together. And you forget, we're on excellent terms, she and I."

That was when her teeth had started chattering. She had managed to say . . . "But my father . . . I mean, if we phone her, we'll have to — "

"Nuts," said Barry. "We'll go see him, after we've seen Mother. I'll carry a tommy gun and a Garand if that will make you feel any better."

Now Abby said, "I can't get over the way your mother took it."

Barry grinned. "I don't know how you knew it," he said, "she was incoherent enough."

Abby said, "It does seem mean . . . not telling her until afterwards. I suppose she's waiting."

"With, I hope, lunch," said Barry cheerfully, "lots of lunch and a shaker. After that, the train, and New York, and tomorrow, the train again." He added gently, "Scared?"

She knew what he meant. She answered

truthfully. "Not with you and never of you, Barry."

As they drove in and parked the car, she saw the other car there and exclaimed, clutching Barry's arm, "That's Craig," she said wildly, "in the car . . . my father must be inside."

"Good!" said Barry. "Keep your chin up. Maybe Mother asked him to lunch too."

Craig, watching, saw them get out of the car. He saw Abby hesitate and turn toward him, saw Barry take her arm. After a moment, they both waved, and went into the house. The door stood open. . . .

Craig thought, She could have spoken to me. . . .

He had lost what he had not had. The loss had been discovered not very long ago. Craig, talking to Morton, the gardener; and Morton saying, "Is that Gambel woman quitting?" He had disliked her always. "Saw her sneaking off at crack of dawn this morning, with a suitcase."

As simple as that, the curiosity aroused, and a little investigation set into motion. It was not hard to find Abby's trunks, packed, locked, the labels reading "Mrs. Barry Lambert" and the New York address.

Mrs. Gambel was leaving presently for Vermont. There were other housekeepers, after all.

So Craig waited while Norman Wallace went

into the Duncan house and, waiting, was rewarded by the glimpse of Abby's anxious face, but not so anxious that the radiance was obscured.

Abby and Barry walked, handfast, into the square hall with its low ceiling and haphazard furniture, and Madge came tearing out of the living room to meet them. Duncan's rather sardonic face was apparent behind her. He merely stood there, grinned a little, and shook his head. . . .

Madge was boiling over, like a geyser. She put her thin arms around them both, she kissed them indiscriminately. She cried, "It's wonderful – though you should both be boiled in oil . . . I'm so excited I can't talk . . . Barry, you crazy idiot . . . Abby, do you think you'll like me? I'm not *really* very likeable. . . ."

Duncan extricated bride and bridegroom from his wife's grip. He kissed one, shook hands with the other. He said, low, "Hadn't you better tell them?"

Madge said, "Oh, I forgot. Abby, your father's here. He's in the little room off the living room. You know, Barry, my office or whatever it is. It seemed just right. Not too friendly. Darlings, he is in a tizzy. He's simply beside himself with rage . . . So I asked him to stay for luncheon and to fetch that poor

Emerson boy in . . . he left him sitting outside like a chauffeur. Really, Abby, he's a most incredible person."

"First impervious man she ever met," said Duncan. He put his hand on Abby's shoulder, and his amiable face showed concern. He said. "He's pretty sore, my dear."

Madge said, "After all, he is only a man!" She put her arm around Abby's waist. She said, "You look — lovely." Her eyes were soft with remembered magic. She was so fortunate a woman, she could always recapture it, she would until she was ninety or dead . . . and not always so vicariously as this. She said, "Come along, you two, and get it over with."

"Just as long," said Barry, "as we don't miss the train tomorrow!"

He took Abby's hand, and Duncan followed. They went through the pleasant living room, with its hodgepodge of chintzes, flowers, furniture and into the small square room which Madge for no good reason called her office. It had once been a farm bedroom. It had a fireplace, a couch, a desk, and some comfortable chairs. Norman Wallace was standing by the fireplace. His eyes, resting on Abby and the big redheaded young man with her, were as expressionless as a snake's.

He said, with a terrifying courtesy, "Could I

ask you to let me speak to my daughter, alone?"

Madge jumped. Then she laughed. This was, to her, excessively comic. Barry was speaking, however, seriously. He said, "She's my wife, Mr. Wallace, I'm staying."

Robert Duncan took Madge's arm. He suggested, and no one listened except Madge, "Suppose we clear out . . . ?"

They cleared. But at the doorway Madge was overtaken by impulse. She said sweetly, "And I do *so* hope you'll stay to luncheon," in the general direction of her son's father-in-law. Duncan hauled her away hastily. But she was still laughing. They heard her light voice trail off: ". . . of course, I'm sorry for her, darling, but Barry will take care of the situation . . . and after all, it's all so ridiculous."

"Exactly," said Norman Wallace, "my feeling." He looked at Abby. "I have dismissed Mrs. Gambel," he said. "I suppose you knew that would happen?"

"I hoped that it wouldn't," she said.

He asked, "What else could you expect? May I inquire your plans? Mrs. Duncan," he added, "does not seem — entirely clear."

He spoke to Abby, but Barry answered.

"We are going to town this afternoon and tomorrow to Hot Springs for two weeks." He said, "We shall then return to my apartment

139

in New York . . . as I am working, in the offices of the Elson Estate."

Wallace laid his arm along the low mantel. He said, "This marriage has been singularly unadvised. You have known one another a matter of days. Abby knows nothing about you."

Abby said clearly, "I know all I need know."

"Nor you," said Wallace, "about her. . . . For your sake as well as hers, I came here — assuming that my daughter would not have the common decency to return with you to her own house — to ask you if she has told you about her mother."

"She has," said Barry promptly, while Abby's heart stumbled and then went on, too fast, by far too fast.

Wallace's gray eyes looked away from the black ones. A little color rose heavily to his face. He asked, "And you have no comment?"

"None," said Barry.

"You accept the responsibility?"

Barry said cautiously, "If there is a responsibility, yes."

"Very well," said Wallace. He dropped his arm to his side. He looked extremely tired. He said, "I acted as I believed best, as any father would. In any circumstances, it would be impossible for me to approve of a marriage undertaken in this fashion. However, I shall send out the usual announcements."

"If only," agreed Barry kindly, "to save your face."

Wallace looked at him. "Quite," he agreed dryly. "I shall naturally make the best of what is, to put it mildly, an unhappy position. Only Abby must understand one thing. She is free to come and go, from what has been her home for many years; and you, as her husband, with her. Any other course would be both absurd and melodramatic."

"As absurd and melodramatic as forbidding me the house before the marriage?" Barry suggested.

"That measure," said Wallace coolly, "seemed both reasonable and practical. But what I intended to say is this: if, for any reason, Abby finds that her extraordinary impulsiveness has led her into a situation from which she wishes to extricate herself, she need not come to me for assistance."

"Oh," said Barry, smiling, "if it's that bad, I'll extricate her myself, Mr. Wallace. It's the least I could do for her." He held Abby's hand very hard and the ring cut into it. It hurt but she did not try to disengage herself. She was smiling. It seemed to her that Barry had made as exquisitely humorous a remark as she had ever heard.

"That's very interesting," said Wallace. He

added, "I understand that you were in the war," as if he had said, "in a zoo."

"Long enough," said Barry, "and while I hate to disappoint you, my discharge is honorable."

Wallace's smile was frosty. He said, "You believe in the strategy of attack."

"I don't know much about strategy," said Barry. "I went in as a private. At various times I became a corporal, even a sergeant . . . but I was always busted back to private again. I came out a sergeant," he added — "probably because I *did* come out."

"Then," said Wallace, "you dislike responsibility? For I assume you have sufficient intelligence for leadership. You so readily assume it now."

"It's a little different," said Barry.

"Is it?" asked Wallace. He thought, This is an extraordinarily stubborn and handsome young man. Handsome was perhaps not the exact word. He was reminded suddenly of Michelangelo's Adam.

He said, with indifference, "When you are back and settled, you will let me know . . . after, of course, Craig and I return from Pinehurst?"

"Father —" Abby began. She took a step forward and Barry released her hand. But without the touch of his flesh against hers she was lost, and stood there, uncertain.

"Well?" asked Wallace, with enormous patience.

She said helplessly, "Nothing. Just that I wish it had not been this way."

"It was your way," he reminded her. He walked toward the door, his shoulders square, his head erect. He said, to Barry, "Please tell your mother I am sorry not to be able to accept her hospitality but I have an appointment this afternoon and it has been rather a trying morning."

They stood aside to let him pass but suddenly Abby flashed into life . . . she had reached the door before her father and was running through the larger room, out into the hall and down the steps to the parked cars. Craig turned, and saw her beside him, her hat a tilted halo, her face flushed. She said, "I couldn't let you go without saying good-bye."

He said, a little formally, "Thanks, Abby." Then his face softened. He added, "You have made an unholy mess of it, haven't you?"

She shook her head. She said, "No. . . ."

"You're happy you're going to be happy?" he asked her with resignation.

"Of course. . . ."

He said, "It might have been – I –"

Abby nodded gravely. "Might have been," she said, "but wasn't. Not for a moment, and not really. I'm sorry, Craig."

"You're not. That's just a phrase, easily spoken."

"I suppose so." She hesitated. "I have always known that my father had no particular feeling for me, Craig. But I believe he has now. I believe he hates me."

He said uneasily, "It's been a shock to him, Abby. Even a – a very demonstrative parent would take this hard, you know. You'll have to make allowances for him."

She said, "It doesn't matter now. It's silly, but because it doesn't I should feel grieved, shouldn't I? But I don't. And that's, somehow, the worst of all."

Her father came up on the other side of the car. He said, "We'll go home now," as if he spoke to a servant, and Craig's color darkened slightly. He looked at Abby, and she stood aside. He said, "Good luck. . . ."

The car drove away, and Abby stood looking after it. Barry came tearing down the steps, caught her up in his arms and carried her back into the house. He said, "What goes on? It's far too soon for the old flame to start burning again!"

"What old flame?" demanded Madge, appearing with her husband. "Not Craig Emerson! Don't tell me, Abby! He's nice, but a little bloodless, don't you think?" she asked, detached. "Oh, do set her down, Barry, and stop laughing, you'll drop her. No wonder," said Madge, "that she fancies herself in love with you, after being shut up for a hundred years with that old —"

"You are speaking," interrupted Barry pontifically, "of the father of the woman I love!"

"So-and-so," said Madge imperturbably, "and Craig too. He's like," she commented, "a pleasant shadow."

Barry set Abby on her feet. He said, "What's all this about lunch?"

"And champagne," said Duncan. "I hauled it up personally from the cellar. Lanson '28, The Widow, heaven bless her, '29, and —"

"Amen," said Barry piously.

Madge said, "Let me take Abby upstairs for a moment."

"Warning and stuff?" asked Barry. "Okay, but be a little restrained, mother. I don't want her jumping, screaming, out of windows."

He saw Abby flush and could have lashed himself for saying it. He caught and held her eyes with his own, trying to tell her, I'm sorry . . . doesn't it prove to you that I don't believe it, when I could forget and say a thing like that?

After a moment, he saw her smile.

He watched them go upstairs and then spoke

to Duncan. "How about a cocktail?"

Madge took Abby into her big sunny bed-room, the big bed tented in white canopies, the dressing table littered with jars and bottles, crystal and silver. She said, "Take down your hair, darling. Literally, if you wish . . . and re-move some of the dust of your elopement from that marvelous little pan."

Abby said, "You're awfully good."

"Sometimes," said Madge complacently, "and sometimes I'm quite the contrary." She waited while Abby vanished into the bathroom and when she came out said, enviously, "With a skin like that I dare say you can *afford* to wash!"

Abby said, "Barry left my suitcase down-stairs." She fished in her handbag for a comb and lipstick. She had taken off her hat and now she freed her hair and let it hang, and combed it, as well as she could with the miniature im-plement and began to coil it again.

"My God," said Madge, staring, "if I had hair like that I —"

"What?"

"Never mind. Ask me in twenty years. I can't believe Barry's married," she said. "I can't be-lieve it."

"In a way," said Abby, "I can't, either."

"I used to think I'd cheerfully scratch the eyes out of any daughter-in-law he would bring me, no matter how many and how often," said Madge. "But I feel exceedingly sentimental and pleased at the moment. He needs . . . you, I think. He's changed," she said, "he's changed very much since his return."

"How?" asked Abby gravely.

"I can't tell you," said Madge, "because you didn't know him before. Oh, he's as much fun as ever, and neither more nor less reckless . . . or is he more," she inquired thoughtfully, "considering today's accomplishment? But there's something new . . . a little hard," she said. "And then, of course," she added, "I've spoiled him."

"I know. He told me so."

"He did?" asked Madge. "You know, he adores me, but he really hasn't any *use* for me . . . so you don't need to be jealous of me, Abby."

"I'm not."

"But you could be," said Madge shrewdly; "you could be jealous of anyone or anything he cared for . . . but I'm not in that picture. I adore him, too, but I have never sacrificed myself or anything else to or for him. I'm an utterly selfish woman in a nice way. Oh, generous as hell when it doesn't cost me anything but a pleasant word or a sum of money. But I've never put myself out for anyone. People come along," she said dreamily, "husbands, lovers . . . and I love them with violence, but I don't martyr myself to them and I find that I fall out of love as easily as in. That didn't apply to Barry's father. He didn't live long enough. As for Barry, I'll always love him, and when you two start quarreling I'll probably take his side . . . unless I have sense enough to keep my mouth shut. Because no matter how fond I grow of you — "

Abby said, "That's all right, Mrs. Duncan."

"Try Madge, for size," said her mother-in-law. She added, "I wish you had seen Val's face when, after Barry phoned and I talked to you both, I told her. Darling, she was furious!"

"Why?"

"Are you doing that on purpose?"

"I'm being cautious," Abby said.

"Fine," said Madge. "As long as you're not really a little dope. She wanted him, of course. It isn't necessary to go into the reasons. There are plenty, one better than the next. Powder your classic nose and let's go down and see if she has returned from a very hasty call she had to make in the village. This," said Madge happily, "ought to be good."

Whether it was good, in Madge's sense, or not Abby never knew. Excitement sustained her through luncheon . . . through the toasts and the laughter, and Val, making funny little faces at her over a glass of champagne. Val, behaving

148

very much as Val had always behaved . . . a little condescending . . . a little amused.

"So romantic," said Val, "you two, going off to the deep end of the swimming pool together. Lucky there was water in it."

She regarded Barry and her brown eyes danced. She said, "You have broken my heart but I forgive you."

Barry stretched his long legs beneath the table. He said cheerfully, "I know a guy who can mend it for you, Val. Next time he gets to town on leave I'll have him call you up."

"Do," said Val, "but first, for the record, tell me what Abby's got that I haven't?"

"I wouldn't know," said Barry, "but whatever it is, I want it."

He looked at his watch. He said, "This is all very well, but Mrs. Lambert and I must be on our way. We have a train to catch."

His mother said, "No, you haven't. You're taking the car. It will use up all the coupons I saved against an emergency . . . but it's a sort of wedding gift. Duncan's going in, he'll drive you . . ." She added, "Speaking of gifts . . . I have a few meager ideas on the subject."

The pearls for Abby. Val sat, a little later, on the big screened porch and watched Madge clasp them about Abby's neck. No one noticed her expression or lack of it, except Robert Duncan, who was, in his way, discerning. "I'll get hold of the original tenant," promised his mother, "and see what can be done. Didn't you tell me she was in San Diego?"

Duncan said lazily. "When I look at my overdraft, I'll give you kids a check."

"And I," said Val, "a fish fork . . . fish forks are always useful."

She saw the round pearls against Abby's throat, she saw the emerald on her hand, and she was consumed with rage. You had a good chance so seldom, especially these days. Each lost was one less.

Presently, she stood beside Madge and watched the car drive off. When they returned to the house, the shadows lay thick and golden on the grass. Madge was saying, "The Waldorf . . . Barry's father and I spent our wedding night at the Waldorf, the old one, of course —"

"How can you be sure?" said Val waspishly.

"You have," said Madge, "a rotten disposition. Come in and have a long drink." She looked at Val without affection but with understanding. She said, "I haven't forgotten."

"Any of them?"

"Any," agreed Madge, "but especially not that one." She put her arm through Val's and they went inside. Later, lifting her glass, she looked at Val. "Better luck next time," she said.

150

"I certainly hope so, and you can't blame me."

"Why shouldn't I? Your headwork is wonderful," said Madge.

Val smiled faintly. She said, "I grow no younger, Madge. I meet very few eligible men. The attractive men, those with any substance, are usually married. I'm tired of my job and too lazy to look for another."

Madge said serenely, "If Barry had married you, I would have wished him luck. He would have needed it, I think. I like you . . . but I'm just as glad that he didn't."

"What does he see in her," inquired Val, "except, of course, her face and her figure and that unlikely hair?"

"Which should be enough," agreed Madge. "But I think he sees more than that. I wonder how much more."

Val asked sharply, "Just what do you mean by that?"

"Nothing," said Madge. "Only, Abby has an expendable heart."

11

At dusk the mountains were blue against the darkening sky; at night they were crowned with stars; and when the sun rose they were as armies marching.

Abby and Barry had a cottage, with a fireplace in the living room. And so small a space seemed inadequate to house as much happiness as was contained there.

Barry felt as if his heart held its breath . . . it seemed incredible to him, a man of ordinary, lusty, ephemeral experience, that any woman was capable of so swift and sweet a response, not alone in her physical being but in the quick response of her mind and spirit, her almost uncanny awareness of his mood.

She had an insatiable curiosity, tinctured with wonder and extending far beyond the limitations of desire and fulfillment. It amused him, yet sometimes, even as he laughed, his mind scowled a little, not angrily, but with dubiety and impatience. He, himself, was as a man divided in two, half of him was unspeakably happy, under a wide sky, under a summer sun, with Abby beside him . . . the lazy days, the long rides on the winding bridle paths, the secret excitement of entering a public room and watching people stop speaking to stare at his wife . . . the people they met, kind, amusing . . . cocktails at six . . . dinner at their small table . . . Abby dancing to a good orchestra, light and close in his arms . . . and at night, alone in the still cottage, Abby speaking to him as from a long mutually dreamed dream.

But the other half knew preoccupations that had nothing to do with the girl he had married. While he and Abby played at being man and wife, they were in reality no more and no less than lovers, for marriage comes later, as he knew. D day had come and gone and good men, young men, living men had gone with it . . . men who laughed and cursed and slogged along the beaches . . . men who had wives, as dear to them as Abby was to him; men who had children too young to remember them, or children never seen . . . and boys too young to have loved.

He asked himself, What am I doing here? as he had asked it before . . . a scar across his ribs, a knee that ached after an hour's ride or twisted suddenly on the golf course . . . why should

153

these keep him safe and unafraid? He tried to tell Abby about it, when she questioned him. She was always questioning him, sometimes in words, sometimes by her silences.

She said, "Darling, you did your share. . . ."

"Share, share," he said irritably, "That's a specious word. What's anyone's share? You can't divide it into portions."

They were sitting on the porch of the cottage and presently they would walk over to the hotel and join some people for drinks. Abby had dressed for dinner, in a long, leaf-green frock. Her clothes were, he thought, diverting, spectacular. She said frequently that she did not like them. When she returned to New York, she said firmly, she would dress as she pleased. She had bought things upon their arrival at the hotel, soft sweaters, bright skirts, and some gay striped cottons. Looking at her tonight, he thought, She dislikes Wallace so much that anything he approved would, of course, be distasteful to her.

He cleared his throat and tried to explain. He said, "Look, honey, it isn't, I suppose, patriotism . . . I mean, duty and all that. I don't even know that I fought for an ideal. All I know is, there was a scrap and I wanted to get into it even if I didn't much like it afterwards, the discipline and the god-awful monotony: I thought, When I get overseas, there won't be *that*. But there was.

154

That's what war is, after you take the flags away and silence the bugles . . . monotony . . . pain and blood and fear but always the monotony. But there's a — a kinship . . . which is not like anything you've known before."

He was silent for a moment. Then he said:

"You work with men, you live and sweat and sometimes die with them. Men you haven't known before, might never have known. Often they are as strange to you as if you spoke a different language. But pretty soon you evolve a language each can understand. So you talk it." He grinned, without merriment. "In my outfit there was a kid from Oklahoma and another from Texas, there was a storekeeper from Vermont and a farmer from Iowa and a guy who would have been teaching at Harvard if he hadn't happened to like being in our history better than teaching it. There was a lanky Jew who worked in a clothing store in Chicago, a guy who'd been a croupier in Las Vegas, and another who was a ballet dancer. You get to know them. You get to like them," he said, "and sometimes to hate them and most often to be bored to insanity with them . . . and it's all mixed up, and part of a pattern. Then you find out that no one will ever be closer to you, or as close —" He broke off and asked, "Abby, what's the matter?"

"Nothing," she told him. She said, "Which

one was Vining?"

He said, startled, "None of those . . . he was just —" how to describe Vining, of whom he preferred not to speak? — "a good guy," he said moderately. "Californian. He hadn't been married long. His father was a druggist in a town in Ross County. Vining didn't like the drug business. He said it stunk. He had a couple of years at college and then quit. He was selling life insurance when he got in. . . ."

Abby thought, I wouldn't have liked Vining. She felt drawn to none — not to the farmer from Iowa, nor to the Jewish lad from Chicago. Some, she knew, were dead; many, Barry might never see again, if they lived. Vining was dead. It was not jealousy, it went far deeper . . . it was not so mean an emotion, nor so passionate. It was the stubborn will to love this man completely, and so completely to be loved by him, that it would be as if neither had existed before their initial meeting.

He said, "I guess it's time to get going . . . the Winslows will be waiting."

"What on earth do you see in them?" she asked idly, coming to sit on the arm of his chair.

He said, surprised, "Don't you like them? They're good fun. He's a swell old boy, if a bit of a stuffed shirt, and she's a riot. She must be twenty years his junior . . . someone said she was an obscure little actress in a stock company. I like them," said Barry.

She said quickly, "Of course, they're very kind."

He said, "Trouble with you, darling, you aren't gregarious and you made the mistake of marrying a man who is."

It was true enough. She said, troubled, "It isn't that I don't like people. Only I haven't had very much to do with them."

He said, "You'll learn. Wait till we get home and the local gentry drop in. You'll have to like most of them, Abby, you won't be able to help it. I've had a hell of a lot of fun in district headquarters . . . also ringing doorbells and getting to know people. They plod up my stairs and I set out the beer and the cheese — if I can get it — and presently the air is blue with smoke and we argue and talk and settle the world's problems." He added, "Wait till you get a load of Hageney, he's the district leader . . . he owns an antique shop and lives above it. What a character. He's the guy who persuaded me that I ought to go to law school."

"Law school?" said Abby, startled.

"I didn't tell you?" asked Barry. "Well, have we had time!" He put his arm around her. "Next fall," he said, "evening classes."

"But *why?*" she asked. "I mean, you never

said you wanted to be a lawyer."

"No more do I," he said. "I don't want to practice, and the whole setup will take years. I never was much of a student . . . but a knowledge of the law is a good weapon and, to mix a metaphor, a springboard into practical politics. Did you think I was going to sit on my fanny and yawn over the affairs of the Elson estate for the next half century? Not me, baby."

She said, after a moment, "But I'll be alone. . . ."

"Sure, and if you had a guy who drank like a fish or wolfed around after women, or wrote books or was an actor or a singer or a traveling salesman you'd be alone too . . . some of the time." He pulled her close and kissed her. He said, "Let's be on our way."

Autumn was a long way off, the summer was before them. She thought, Perhaps he will change his mind and he'll just forget about it, after a while.

So they went to the cocktail party. The Winslows were amusing, Barry had a wonderful time, and Abby looked fabulous, and Winslow smote Barry on the back and said, "Oh, boy, are you lucky!"

He thought he was; he thought himself the most fortunate of men . . . yet he was by no means insensitive. Before they left for New

York he was beginning to be aware of a quality in Abby's love for him that was faintly disturbing. He could not name it. If he had, he might have called it devouring, only that would seem an incongruous term to use of her. But there it was, and it had nothing to do with the give-and-take of passion . . . it was not so easily dismissed.

He had believed that, if there was a flaw in her, she lacked humor . . . as indeed she might, considering the life she had led. But he found, to his delight, that he was mistaken. She had humor, very much her own. It was not ribald, nor earthy, nor of the sort that finds amusement in the discomfiture of others. There was nothing sardonic about Abby, nor unkind, and she was blind to satire. But humor was there, subtle, mischievous, and very unexpected. She had, perhaps, had little occasion to exercise it before. But now, as she was happy, she could laugh.

He thought, a hundred times a day, and his mind rapped wood, God, I'm lucky.

So when the faint disturbance troubled him . . . he brushed it aside. The honeymoon scales of emotion maintain a very delicate balance. Abby was younger in many ways than her years. She had been unhappy for a long time. All this he knew, as he rationalized the things that made him uneasy. There was little he did not know about Abby, now. She gave him her past life as though it were a trivial gift, which he could regard and throw away. In return, she wanted his. It made him uncomfortable, the questioning, the gentle probing. Not that there was anything to hide, but he felt like a damned fool, talking about things that had happened so long ago they might as well have happened to someone else.

For the most part he was patient with her, more patient than anyone who had known him would suspect he could be. But he was puzzled. And once, when she asked him about Val — "How did you feel about her, were you attracted by her?" — he was amused but irritated.

"Look, brat," he said, "you told me once you didn't want to know about my girls."

"She was your girl?"

"Don't be so quick on the uptake. Good Lord, no . . . But, when we were driving back after our marriage . . ."

She said, "I don't want to know *then*," She colored, and turned her face away. And looking at her, he laughed. He said, "I see. . . ."

"Perhaps," she said. "But Val . . . after all, I *know* Val, I knew her long before you did."

He said carelessly, "She's damned attractive . . . I was curious about her. Perhaps, if you hadn't come along. . . ."

She asked, breathless, "You would have married Val?"

"Who said anything about marriage?" he demanded.

"Oh," said Abby, in a small voice, and he added, wickedly, not because he had any wish to hurt her but because it seemed funny to him, "And now I'll never know."

"What?"

"What I was curious about. Come on, it's lunch time and I'm starved."

They were riding, the rest of the party far ahead. It was a crazy conversation to conduct on horseback, anyway. . . . Barry's horse brushed past Abby's and they were ahead. Barry shouted, "Beat you in . . . " and the conversation ended.

But she did not forget it. That night, lying awake, beside him, she thought of Val. He'd been attracted by Val, but he hadn't wanted to marry her. Had he wanted to sleep with her, what had he wanted of her, what about her had made him — curious? In itself, an odd word, she thought. She was suddenly savagely angry with Val, for existing and with Barry, who had, after a fashion, called her into existence.

Yes, with Barry most of all. Because she couldn't know what he thought: she couldn't creep into his mind; she couldn't know what he felt: she couldn't get inside his blood and flesh and bones. She could not see Val through Barry's eyes because she, Abby, was not Barry. She was another person. She was herself, and did not wish to be.

He woke and felt her hands on him, the long fingers tracing the scar along his ribs, he heard her shaken breath.

He sat straight up in bed, and shook the good, heavy sleep from his red head. He said, "Hey, what's all this about?"

"I'm sorry," she said stifled.

Barry reached out his hand and switched on the bedside light. He saw her face, he saw the heavy braids of hair, the flawless line of throat and cheek. He saw her tears, which did not disfigure her.

He said, holding her, "What is it, Abby . . . a nightmare?"

A nightmare . . . a dreadful nightmare . . .

She said, shuddering, "You — one day you'll die, Barry, or I — one of us. . . ."

"Well, sure," he said, "in forty or fifty years."

"It's too short," she said, "however long it may be. . . ."

He cradled her in his arms, pulling her across his knees, her head on his shoulder. The quiet night pressed against the windows and the stars looked down.

After a while she stirred, smiled, and reached up to touch his cheek with her head. She said again, "I'm sorry."

"Should be," he told her, "waking me up. I was having a wonderful dream."

"Was I in it?"

"As a matter of fact, you weren't. I was batting around in a plane, Madge at the controls. I had six bottles of beer and a hamburger and I was singing 'Old Pilots Never Die'!"

"Were you really?"

"No," he admitted; "if you must know, I wasn't dreaming anything. I was out cold."

She said, "All right. I'll let you go back to sleep." She asked, "I wonder if all brides behave like this?"

"I hope not," he said piously, "as they don't all have kind, understanding husbands."

He leaned to kiss her and presently she said, "I wasn't being morbid . . . it was just . . . I began to think, that someday, somewhere, it must end."

"Why?" he asked gently.

"Do you believe that?" she demanded.

He was embarrassed, suddenly. There were beliefs that were not so much beliefs as something rooted in you, something you could not explain. He said, "Sure."

"I don't," she said. "I think — not to go on —

always, forever and together!"

He said, "You do go on, in your children, Abby, and your grandchildren."

"Grandchildren?" She laughed, a lovely sound in the night. She could not see herself as a grandmother. But the laughter died. She whispered, "Have you forgotten?"

"Of course not." He took the heavy braids in his hand, weighing them. He said, "As soon as we get back we'll start to track down Gilpin or whatever his name was. Wasn't he a highwayman, by the way? Stop worrying. We'll have six kids and every one of them will be able to lick me by the time he's nine."

Abby was not listening now. She said, after a moment, "If I thought you belonged to me, Barry, as I do to you. . . ."

Sooner or later you have to learn; some people are born with the knowledge, some learn the hard way, and some, imperceptibly, by degrees.

He said quietly, "Abby, if by belonging you mean ownership, no one ever owns anyone . . . ever. . . ."

She said, "I suppose not," and turned away from him, and presently he slept, quickly, the deep, healthy sleep, and she was quiet beside him in the big bed.

It was not true; it could not be . . . he loved

her . . . as no one had ever loved her, as she had not dared dream she might be loved. More, she loved him, to the utter exclusion of anything or anyone else. She did belong to him, he did own her. That much was true. If that was true, then why —?

She said, "Barry?" and again, "Barry. . . ."

But he slept and did not answer. And a new fear nagged at her again, nibbling like a rodent at the edges of her brain. She could wake him, this time, and make him answer. Someday she would not be able to wake him.

But that day was a lifetime away, she had his reassurance and that of her own common sense. There was an even deeper fear, which had come from shock.

No one owns anyone . . . ever.

No one belongs. . . .

She put her hand on him lightly, so that he would not wake. His flesh was as familiar to her as her own. Yet he lay sleeping, his integrated self shut away from her. She had no real knowledge of him beyond the flesh. She was wife to a stranger.

12

There is no private heaven. No matter how securely and secretly you build your personal paradise, there are always gate crashers or those who hold priority cards of admission.

And if, as is customary, you build your Eden for two, one usually wants out . . . if only temporarily.

Barry was a gregarious animal. He and Abby arrived in New York in a sweltering heat wave, and Barry went happily back to work. He had had enough of relaxing. Once, he had believed that to sit in the sun, the guns silenced, the stench and misery a bad dream, would be enough. But it was not enough, even with such a companion as Abby.

The little flat was hotter than the gates of perdition . . . the asphalt melted in the streets; people sat on the old-fashioned brownstone stoops and quietly melted . . . but Barry's vitality was unimpaired.

Madge had, in some measure, rejuvenated the apartment; heat wave or not, it was a pleasant place and in the evenings they could sit out on the flat roof with its grimy parapet, its one rusty little cedar in the faded blue wooden tub. But they rarely sat there alone. The entire neighborhood dropped in, to welcome Barry home and to meet his bride.

She could not understand his interest in these people, who seemed commonplace to her ... men and women, young or elderly, who had little jobs and led a little existence; housewives, tradespeople ... Even Hageney, the district leader, did not appear to her as the special person of whom Barry had told her so much, so enthusiastically. He was a little man, dry as dust.

They had a common meeting ground, however; Hageney knew nothing about paintings and cared less, but he had an expert's knowledge of antiques. His specialty was early American, but he liked Chinese porcelains and he and Abby could talk while Barry listened. Hageney, looking at Abby with his sagacious old eyes, said bluntly, "She isn't politically minded but that won't matter ... there'll come a day when she'll get up on a platform and the voters will just look at her and it will be in the bag."

When he or others came Abby made herself

useful, bringing cold drinks out on the roof, sitting beside Barry, listening to the discussions. It was imperative for her to know and comprehend these people if they were so important to Barry.

Her household duties were miniature in the extreme. Barry applauded her cooking, her efficiency, her triumphant battle with ration books, but he was not content to retire into domestic life. They went out, a good deal. He liked to exhibit her, and said so. He was amused when a columnist saw them at a roof garden, a night club or a theater and wrote about them: "Barry Lambert, the extraordinary Madge Duncan's extraordinary son, back from the wars with the reward of all good soldiers, medals, an honorable discharge and a beautiful wife . . . New York has not before had the opportunity to see much of Mrs. Lambert, who is the daughter of the legendary Norman Wallace. . . ."

Weekends, they went to Fairton to be with Madge. But it was not until the end of the summer, during a sultry August, that Abby saw her father.

They had gone, Friday afternoon, to Madge's . . . where they would be alone, for once, Madge said, over the telephone. The guests she had expected hadn't reached New York from California . . . bumped off the plane some-

168

where improbable, she said sadly. Madge liked a houseful. She invited people with reckless abandon, all kinds of people, and then, when they appeared, seemed mildly astonished, leaving them to their own devices and to her husband, who as host was spectacularly successful.

In the train, "I'm glad there won't be anyone else," said Abby.

Barry yawned, and looked out at the dusty trees, the leaves limp in the unstirring air. He asked, "Why? I was looking forward to your meeting the Petersens, they're swell people."

Abby said, "We're hardly ever alone."

Barry grinned. He said, "You're too exclusive . . . I supposed you'd settle for a desert island?"

"Sometimes," said Abby, "I think I would. When does the next canoe leave for Tahiti?"

"Wednesday nights, at nine, but you'll go alone, my girl. The South Sea Island story was always a fable."

"No," said Abby, "you wouldn't like it."

"Check," said Barry. "I'd have the hell bored out of me a week from last Monday."

Abby was silent, looking from the windows of the car, which needed washing. She thought, Well, this is the way it's going to be. . . .

He asked, "Are you going to see your father?"

Abby turned back to him. She had lost a little weight during the weeks in town and her pallor was marked and luminous; her eyes were bright against it and her rouged mouth. She asked, "Why should I?"

"Wasn't that the idea, eventually?"

Abby shrugged. "If so, not mine," she said.

Barry said presently, "Personally, if I never see him again I'll survive . . . but it seems a little foolish doesn't it? After all," he said casually, "he's an old man."

Abby said, with tightened lips, "I thanked him for his wedding present."

Barry took her hand. It was cold, suddenly. He said, low, "I thought you weren't going to let that throw you, darling."

"I'm not," she said.

Norman Wallace had sent them the portrait of his wife. Barry remembered the hot still night he had come home to find it there, still crated, and had uncrated it, sweating copiously in his shirtsleeves. He remembered Abby's bitter whisper. "He sent it as a reminder."

She had refused to hang it. It was back in the crate, in the storeroom.

He said gravely, "Abby, we've tried and failed. Dr. Gilpin is dead, we can't trace his assistants at the time of your birth . . . nor his records. The only way to the truth is through your father . . . but you will never get it by antagonizing him further."

She said unhappily, "What brings this up, all of a sudden?"

"Emerson phoned me," he said uncomfortably, "yesterday, at the office. He asked me to have a drink with him before I went home. So I did . . . and he said it was important. . . ."

Abby asked, "But not important enough to tell me, last night." But he saw that, however unwillingly, her interest was aroused.

He said, "I met him at the Ritz . . . we had a drink or two. He told me your father isn't very well. He also said that Val Stanley is not working this summer. She's been living with her people in Fairton and spending most of her time at your house."

"Val!"

"Yep." He grinned. "Emerson," he said, "is a good little guy. And he's afraid that Val has designs on the old man."

"I don't believe it," said Abby blankly.

The train snorted and slowed. The conductor came through and announced nasally, "Fairton . . . Fairton . . ." and Barry rose, made a long arm, and took their luggage from the rack.

Madge was waiting in the station wagon; wearing a slack suit, impeccably tailored, her rusty-red hair bound back from her little face with a ribbon.

Barry put the bags in the back, and they

171

climbed in and sat in front with Madge.

"Hi, kids," said Madge. "Abby, you look a little washed out. Never mind, you'll have enough rest this weekend . . . Bob and I play gin rummy and look at each other. The pool's been emptied and refilled. My God, what weather! I'd welcome a blizzard."

"Take that back," said Barry, "or it will be remembered against you next winter."

Madge asked, "How's the city, and my friend Hageney? I must have him up here," she said dreamily, turning a corner on a wheel and a half. "Love that man . . . the night I dropped in and found you surrounded by the good neighbors I felt as if I had walked into a Saroyan set."

Barry said gravely, "Hageney approved of you too. He said, if you had been properly brought up and decently educated you might have been a reasonably valuable individual."

Madge was delighted. She said, "I bet he says that to all the girls . . . I must have him," she added firmly, "bring him up some weekend."

"There's a Mrs. Hageney," said Barry.

"Bring her too," said Madge; "what's she like?"

"Like nothing on earth," said Abby. "She's tremendously fat . . . and she knits. . . ."

"Sounds like the White Queen," said Madge, "maybe it's just shawls."

"Mrs. Hageney," said Barry agreeably, "has a Ph.D. and she's a very astute character. They haven't been married very long. She lived abroad a good deal . . . after she gave up teaching."

Abby cried, "You never told me. . . ."

"Thought you might find it out for yourself," said Barry.

"Knits?" repeated Madge thoughtfully. "Do I hear a tumbrel roll? I warn you. Barry, when I do, I shall mount it clad in chinchilla and emeralds."

They were turning into the driveway. Abby took off her little hat and lifted her face to a small, dry breeze. It was pleasant to be coming back, to a big cool room, with the smell of roses and the sound of trees stirring . . . to the pool, and lazy mornings.

"You look lousy," said Madge mildly, to her daughter-in-law. "Why don't you stay here with us? Barry can come up weekends."

Barry said, "She wouldn't leave me, would you, Abby?"

"No," said Abby, smiling.

"Well," Madge said, and braked to a startling stop as Duncan came lounging out to meet them. "I'll suggest it again next summer, when the bloom has worn off. Nip upstairs, take off some clothes and we'll have something to drink on the terrace and a cold supper. . . ."

Abby stood by the bedroom window, looking over the lawn running back to the fields checkerboarded with stone walls. Barry came up and put his arm around her. "Ready to go down?" he asked.

She said, "Yes, of course. . . ." She turned and put her cheek against his breast. She said, "Tomorrow, I'll go up to the house. . . ."

He knew what house she meant. He asked curiously, "Because of Val?"

"In a way," she said truthfully. "It makes me —" she stopped and laughed — "mad, I suppose," she concluded, "irritated at any rate, and very curious."

He said, "Emerson's a dope. There's probably nothing to it . . . if there were, however, he'd have reason to worry about his status."

"Nonsense," said Abby, "he's too necessary to Father. But Val . . ." She drew a deep breath. "I don't understand it," she said.

Later that evening, when Bob and Barry had disappeared, to walk around the pool and smoke, and she and Madge were alone on the terrace, Abby asked directly, "Have you seen anything of Val Stanley?"

Madge said cautiously, "Now and again. She's staying up here this summer . . . she comes over and swims."

Abby said, "Barry saw Craig in town, yesterday. He told him that Val is spending a lot of time — " she hesitated and then said — "viewing the Wallace Collection."

Madge said, "Well, you'd discover it sooner or later. I understand she's taking a most intelligent interest in art. I met her aunt at Red Cross last week. *She* said Val is working for your father."

"Working?" said Abby, in astonishment.

Madge said mildly, "She was a secretary before she became a model."

"I'd forgotten," said Abby.

Madge asked, "Do you mind?"

"No," said Abby. Then, "Yes, I do mind . . . mainly, I think, because I don't understand. I never knew Val very well but it would seem to me that she doesn't do anything without a motive."

Madge said, "There's talk in the village, of course . . . Some people say, they wonder now that you've . . . well, left him, so to speak, if he'll remarry."

"That's absurd."

"What is?" asked Barry, coming up behind her, quietly.

She said "Madge was just saying that there's gossip about Father and Val Stanley . . . that people even wonder if he'll marry her."

Barry fell into a long chair. "How fascinating — and revolting," he commented.

"And unlikely," said Bob Duncan. "Wallace is too smart."

"Could be," said Madge brightly, "a species of revenge. You married," she reminded her daughter-in-law, "and against his wishes . . . Val likes the fleshpots. There aren't too many eligible men around at the moment and frankly, darling, your father can't live forever."

"My advice," said Bob practically, "not that you asked for it, angel, is to get yourself up there, but fast, and reinstate yourself in the parental graces, thus cutting the ground from beneath the Stanley feet . . . unless you wish a depleted inheritance."

She said indifferently, "I expect that anyway . . . and as long as Barry doesn't care, I don't."

Barry said, "The little woman is the least mercenary of females. But at the same time," he added, "she doesn't like to have her eye wiped by the lovely companion of her recent youth. Isn't that it in, to coin a phrase, a nutshell?" He added, "The spectacle of Val endeavoring to add herself to the collection is alarming."

"Old master," murmured Madge, "or new mistress. . . ."

Her son said austerely, "That will be all from you."

"Why?"

He said, "If I know our Val she would hold out for the legalities and I rather suspect that my dear father-in-law is not interested in Restoration comedy."

"Do you remember Albert?" Madge asked her husband.

"What a mind!" said Bob. "Albert who?"

"I don't remember his surname," said Madge impatiently. "He was a sweet old thing in a sinister sort of way. We met him in Paris . . . surely you remember . . . he was seventy-four. . . ."

"Ah," said Bob brightening, "I do remember . . . and she — what was her absurd name . . . Poppy, wasn't it? She was nineteen."

Madge said, "He wouldn't marry her because she wasn't quite his alleged class. But he acknowledged the twins."

"Twins?" said Barry, and shouted with laughter.

"No laughing matter," said Madge severely.

Abby rose. She said, "I'm tired, a little . . . mind if I go in? Not you, Barry," she said, "you stay out here, it's cooler . . . but I'm so sleepy. . . ."

Madge said, "I'll come up with you."

She came into the bedroom and looked at

Abby. She asked, "I've offended you?"

"About father and Val?" Abby sat down on the bed. "No," she said, "of course not, but I can't believe it."

Madge said gently, "Why not, dear? Do be realistic . . . True, he's over seventy – but . . . Val's a remarkably attractive girl and I dare say quite unscrupulous. She'd put up with a good deal to be Mrs. Norman Wallace . . . for a while, at any rate. Afterwards, well," she prophesied vaguely, "money, position, and a chance to meet a great many men she might not otherwise encounter."

"If," said Abby painfully, "my father contemplated any such step it would be because . . ." She swallowed. This was very hard to say. She went on, flushing under Madge's black eyes, so like Barry's, "He's always hated . . . sex."

"He married," said Madge, "and you were born."

"I think," said Abby, "it wasn't so simple as that. My mother . . . you heard Barry joke about Val's becoming part of the collection? My mother did become just that . . . the . . . the other relationship was quite secondary. I feel certain . . . I suppose, however, he wanted a son, a sort of – dynasty business."

"Then," said Madge, startled, contemplating a type of man she did not know existed, normally, "if he married Val — ?"

"It would be as you yourself said," said Abby, "because he wanted to hurt me."

Barry came leaping up the stairs and crashed into the room. He took his little parent by her thin shoulders. "Get the hell out of here," he said genially, "your husband wants someone to play gin rummy with him. He is quietly drinking himself to death and there are mosquitoes on the terrace. Besides, I want a word with the current Mrs. Lambert."

When Madge had gone and the door had closed, he took Abby in his arms. "Don't think about it, it's pretty damned silly."

"Val? I'm not so sure."

"You don't like it, do you?"

"No . . ." She looked at him, her face strained and quiet. She said, "I can't believe it . . . but it does hurt."

He said gently, "Not you . . . you're a tenacious wench. Shall you get over loving me, Abby?"

"No."

No protestations. Just the denial.

"And there's nothing I could do . . ." He stopped, watching her face. "If I were unkind," he asked, "if I were unfaithful?"

Her face changed, a very little. She said, "Not even then."

"It looks," he said, "as if I were saddled with you, for life." He kissed her. He said, after a minute, "Stop worrying. . . ."

She said, "I'm not. Just — thinking. Will you drive me —" she hesitated — "home, tomorrow?"

13

It was a curious homecoming. When they drove up, Craig was standing outside talking to Morton, the sullen gardener. He looked at the car, at Abby as she got out, his eyes widening . . . He came forward, and took her hands in his. He said, "You don't know how glad I am to see you."

He looked, she perceived, a little haggard.

Barry asked, "Can I leave the car here? Good! I told you I'd deliver her, Emerson. She's a very docile girl. I merely issue orders. I said, 'Abby, you are to pay your respects to your father.' "

Abby said, "He loves to hear himself talk." She put her hand on Craig's arm and he looked down at her. He thought, She is lovelier than ever. Barry, standing there in the sun, regarding them from his great height, his red head high, was the personification, Craig thought enviously, of arrogance; a man to whom the good things came easily.

He wished in his heart that he had not telephoned Barry, had not made it clear that Abby must contemplate the situation for herself. He had not seen her since her marriage. He could, he had thought, forget her, after a fashion . . . go on, with what was left, and what the future would hold; security, at least, and freedom to do as he pleased with that security.

But as he no longer felt secure he had run to Barry Lambert in his uncertainty.

Abby asked, "Father home?"

"Wait a minute," said Craig, "before you go in . . . I want to talk to you about something. . . ."

She shook her head. "Val, you mean? There isn't anything to talk about, is there?"

He said desperately, "But there is . . . it's serious, I tell you, Abby, anything might happen."

She asked quietly, "If so, what makes you think that I could prevent it?"

He began to stammer in his earnestness. He said, "But you could . . . I mean if you'd . . ." He stopped, in despair, he didn't know what he had been going to say.

Abby said, "Perhaps you'd like me to divorce Barry and come home?" She smiled, genuinely amused. "But that's one thing I can't do," she added, "even though he does beat me regularly and runs around with other women." She watched Craig's altering face, and laughed. "I forgot," she said, "you weren't there when Father told us that if I decided I had made a mistake, I needn't come running home to him!"

Craig made a defeated gesture. He said, "I don't know what to say, except that if you and Uncle Norman could be friends again, it might make a difference."

She asked softly, "And when were we ever friends?"

Barry spoke, looking from one to the other. "I can understand your — interest, Emerson. And naturally, Abby's interested too — but she has nothing at stake."

Craig regarded him with acute dislike. He turned to Abby and said, with some formality, "If you'll come in . . . ? Uncle Norman's in the library — he's had an air-conditioning unit put in . . . as he works there a good deal, with," he explained evenly, "Val."

"Maybe you'd better prepare him," said Abby, as evenly.

The hall was cool and still, the Holbein portrait looked down from above the fireplace . . . the library door was closed. Craig knocked, and Abby was aware of a sharp twinge of revulsion. Craig so rarely knocked on that particular door.

He went in, and a moment later opened the door, and beckoned them. Norman Wallace rose from behind his desk. Barry, regarding him, thought that Craig's announcement that his employer had not been well lately must have been a decoy. Wallace looked remarkably well.

So did Val, as sultry as the weather, yet extraordinarily demure . . . in a bright gypsy skirt, full, doll-waisted; a white, sheer blouse threaded with a black velvet ribbon. Barry's eyes went swiftly to Abby's and then he turned them away . . . they could laugh together later.

"My dear Abby," said Wallace pleasantly, "this is a surprise!" He took her hands lightly and his were dry and cool.

Val said, "Hello, Abby. . . ." Her dark eyes moved slowly over Barry. "Hi," she said, smiling, and putting her notebook on the table.

Wallace said, "I've been hoping you would come. I dare say, however, you have been very busy." He looked at Craig, and said, "They'll lunch, of course."

Abby started to speak and Barry kicked her sharply in the ankle. He spoke for them both, with moderate enthusiasm. "We'd like to, sir," he said.

"Fine," said Wallace genially. "It's too warm for sherry," he said, "but I have some excellent rum."

Val rose. She said easily, "Never mind, Craig . . . I'll speak to Mrs. Renning. This *is* fun," she added, and went from the room

184

with her model's walk.

Craig was a little white. Wallace explained, "Mrs. Renning is Mrs. Gambel's successor. Valentine found her for me, in Litchfield. She's quite adequate." He added, "Suppose we go out on the sun porch . . . ?"

Val joined them there presently and sat down beside Wallace, by which time the small talk had been exhausted. . . . Had they enjoyed their trip? How was Mrs. Duncan? He had heard, of course, that they had been coming up weekends and hoped to see them . . . but hardly liked to intrude.

Now he said, "Valentine's been literally a lifesaver, Abby. She is getting the notes into shape . . . a publisher —" he turned to Barry, "perhaps you know him, Anderson —? was here last weekend, talking things over with me. I had intended to publish the book privately but he has persuaded me against it."

"Of course," said Val firmly, "it's silly for Norman not to share it with a great many people, and besides, there's a definite market for autobiographies, especially of this kind."

"She's very practical," said Wallace, smiling thinly.

"I know Evan Anderson," said Val casually, "and so, when I ran into him in town. . . ."

The elderly manservant appeared with the

rum collinses . . . His old eyes lighted when he saw Abby and she rose and went to speak to him.

"How are you, Peters?" she asked. "It's nice to see you."

He said he was fine. He added, low, and his mouth shook a little, "We've missed you Miss — I mean, Mrs. Lambert."

When he had gone Val scrubbed industriously at the tray with a bright cocktail napkin. She said, "Peters is getting unsteady, I'm afraid, poor soul."

Luncheon was good, cool, with salads and iced shrimp, and a little stately. There was, to Abby's astonishment, sauterne for those who cared for it. Her father drank several glasses, but then he had not taken the rum. His eyes grew bright, and a little wavering.

After luncheon he asked, "Abby, would you come to the library with me for a moment . . . if Barry and Valentine will excuse us? I have something for you."

She followed him, feeling acutely uncomfortable; her throat dry and tight. She was utterly bewildered; by the change in him, and, in a lesser degree, by Val . . . Val had called him Norman, as easily as she called Barry by his given name. Val who, taking over from Craig, gave the orders in the house.

Wallace was unlocking the door to the wall safe set in behind the books, which he pulled out and heaped on the desk. He fiddled with the dial and the safe itself swung open. He removed a big jewel case, put it on the desk and opened it. He said, "These are yours, Abby. I should, I suppose, have sent them with the portrait but I am still sentimental enough to wish to give them to you personally." He lifted the top of the box and the trays slid out. The jewelry was there, each piece in place, a good deal of it; all of it old and of an exquisite workmanship.

He said superfluously, "Your mother's. It became her, as it will you. The intrinsic value, that is to say, of the stones, is not of any moment. But the workmanship and the antiquity —"

Garnets, wide bracelets, earrings, a brooch . . . flawed emeralds and darkened pearls in breathtaking patterns . . . wonderful old paste . . . sapphires set in delicate enamel. . . .

He said, "I want you to have everything of hers."

On the surface a charming sentence and, as he had said, sentimental. But the gray eyes were not bright and wavering now . . . they were like dulled steel and as hard.

Abby said, after a moment, "Thank you, father."

"Not at all. Sit down, Abby." And when she had done so he said, "You could have come before. . . ."

She said, "You didn't indicate that you wished me to come."

"I thought I had . . . during that painful interview at your mother-in-law's house. I said very clearly, that we would observe the amenities."

Abby put out her hand and picked up a ring . . . blue enamel with a circle of onyx, and in the center a star sapphire, the diamonds around it worn almost flat.

She asked directly, "What is Val Stanley doing here?"

A swift look of pleasure altered her father's face but she did not see it, she was looking at the ring again.

"Haven't I explained sufficiently?"

"No. . . ."

Mr. Wallace rose. He said easily:

"My dear Abby! Surely it is obvious that Valentine is a charming young person and that I enjoy her companionship. She is intelligent, she has a quick grasp . . . it has been a pleasure" — he smiled a little — "to . . . shall we say? . . . complete her education. Also, she has been most helpful to me. You, I may remind you, left me more or less stranded."

She said stubbornly, and her eyes blazed blue, "Craig is perfectly capable of working on the book . . . he always was."

"Quite," agreed Wallace, "but he has other duties to perform."

She said, "You — didn't like her; you said once she was not — the friend you would select for me."

"I apologize," said her father. "I had seen little of her since her childhood." He smiled at her. "Take the jewelry," he said, "and we'll join Valentine and Barry. . . ."

They had remained in the sun porch, Val in a long chair. The striped skirt exposed her lovely long legs and her excellent ankles. Barry stood smoking by the fireplace, which had been filled with white birch logs.

When Abby and Wallace had left them, Barry asked, "What are you up to, Val?"

"What makes you think I am up to anything?"

He said, "Nuts to that, darling. Why this sudden obsession with art? Surely, not for art's sake?"

She said warily, but smiling, "I find it intensely interesting."

Barry laughed. She amused him, even now,

when he was annoyed and angry, for Abby's sake.

He asked, "Are you trying to marry my revered father-in-law?"

The dark, vivid face did not change. She said lazily, "It's an idea. . . ."

"A fairly repulsive one," agreed Barry.

"How flattering." She opened her eyes wide. She added, "Would you explain that . . . or, maybe you'd better not?"

It's an odd thing; there are women so female that a man can speak brutally and be understood. Barry said, "It would be a quaint but not unusual form of prostitution."

Her full mouth tightened. But her voice was under control.

"Thanks, too much," she said. She sat up and looked at him. "See here," she went on, "are you being nasty just for fun or are you afraid that Abby will lose out?"

"How like you," he commented; "but as long as we are talking facts, no, I'm not afraid. I don't give a good goddam; I have enough money. . . ."

"Yes," she said, with mock sorrow, "so you have." She shrugged. "I don't see why I owe you any explanation — however, I grow no younger, and eligible men are hard to come by. I meet only married men, for the most part. . . ."

"Don't tell me that would deter you!"

"Frankly, no," said Val placidly, "but so far I haven't met one worth the effort, or the repercussions." She smiled and added, "Abby would be affronted, wouldn't she, if she realized that it's your fault?"

"Mine!" But he was not so astonished as he appeared and she knew it.

"Providing," she said lazily, "that I do bring it off." She rose and came to stand by him, close. She wore a little perfume, not too much, of a heady sweetness. She said dreamily, "You have everything, you know . . . suitable . . . exciting and — as you just admitted . . . you even have money. But, unhappily, you weren't in love with me."

Barry was not embarrassed. Val might annoy or anger but she couldn't embarrass him.

He said, "No. . . ."

"You might have been," she said, "if Abby hadn't appeared at the swimming pool, all eyes and hair and innocence."

"I might," he said grimly, "yet I doubt that it would have endured as far as the altar."

She said, laughingly, "I would have held out for the altar, Barry, and it's entirely possible that you —"

He shook his head, with violence. He said, "Come off it, Val."

"We'll never know, now," she said sadly.

Barry moved away from her. He said, "So you'd marry that old fossil for the collection, which by the way has been left to the Metropolitan Museum, I understand . . . and this barracks of a house, and what money there is in it. . . ."

"Any objection?"

"None, whatever, except the natural and impersonal reaction of any guy contemplating such a spectacle, plus the fact that I don't want Abby hurt."

"Why should she be?" asked Val, entertained. "As you have nobly said, you don't care about dower rights."

He said, "She'll be hurt . . . I think . . . and if she is. . . ."

"What," asked Val, "can you do about it . . . now?"

She broke off, hearing steps. Wallace came through to the sun porch with Abby. She was carrying the jewel case.

Wallace looked from Barry to Val and smiled. Everything was going according to strategy, he thought complacently. He said easily, "I have given Abby her mother's things."

Val cried, "Oh, may I see them?"

Abby set the case down on a table and opened it, and Val came to look and exclaim. Barry

192

looked too, recognizing the delicacy of the pieces, the rings and brooches, the earrings and necklaces and bracelets. He said, pleased, "They're beautiful."

"Yes," said Abby, and touched the dimmed glitter with a careful hand. She was pale, her husband saw. He put his arm around her, and asked, "Shouldn't we be going back? Madge said something about . . . people for tea. . . ."

She had said nothing of the kind. Abby leaned back against him, gratefully . . . And Wallace watching, spoke:

"I wanted Abby to have these trinkets . . . they are hers, rightfully, as Val has already agreed. . . ."

Barry's arm tightened about Abby. Wallace went on, without a perceptible break, "Val will of course have her own jewelry . . . of a type more − suitable." He put out his hand and took Val's. "I am glad you came today. This seems as good a time as any to tell you that Val and I are to be married, very soon."

Someone said something, stifled. It sounded like "My God!" Craig had come in quietly and was standing by the door. Wallace turned. He said, "My dear boy, do come in . . . not that this announcement can be much of a surprise to you."

Val said, "No one looks particularly astonished or enthusiastic."

"You can't," Wallace agreed reasonably, "blame them. I am an old man, Valentine, and you are very young woman."

"History," said Barry politely, "keeps repeating itself. Congratulations, Mr. Wallace."

Abby had not spoken. Her father said mildly, "That's handsome of you, Barry."

He released Val's hand and walked over to Abby. He asked, "And you, Abby?"

He was shaken suddenly by her resemblance to her mother. But there was more spirit here, more stamina. She looked at him and smiled. She said, "No, I'm not exactly astonished father . . . and I hope you and Val will be very happy."

Craig made another stifled sound and went from the room. Val looked after him, her eyebrows raised. She said, "Craig seems upset."

She went over to stand by Wallace. She looked at Barry a moment and then bent to kiss Abby's cheek. "You don't mind having me for a stepmother, darling?" she asked.

"No," said Abby and added, "I don't mind anything."

Her father commented: "What a curious way to put it . . . a week from today, then, and here . . . I'll expect you and Barry . . . Just the family," he added, "and of course, Valentine's. We are going to Maine for a short stay . . . and

194

shall then return here."

Val said, "Barry, do let go of Abby. I'm sure she isn't going to fall without your support." She put her own arms around Abby and Abby stood quietly within the warm circle. She said coaxingly, "I know it's been a shock . . . but, darling, will you be my — what is it? — matron of honor?"

In a gown fashioned as her mother's had been, with her mother's jewels . . . two could play at reminding. . . .

Abby said, "I would like to, very much."

When they were in the car, Barry swore fluently and continuously from the house to the gates, while Abby listened with admiration and interest. As they turned out of the drive she said respectfully, "Congratulations. I've never even *heard* some of them before."

Barry laughed, "Sorry darling," he said, "but of all the unmitigated, brassbound, hell-bent —"

Abby said, "Hey . . . enough's enough. First thing you know you'll be repeating yourself."

He said grimly, "I understand that your pa has a fine collection of jade. Well, he's bought himself quite a specimen."

"Look," asked Abby, "are you mad because of me, Barry, or because you don't like seeing a girl Val's age marry a man over seventy or because it's Val who is marrying him?"

"How very involved, Mrs. L."

She said patiently, "Answer me, Butch."

Barry pondered. The slight breeze engendered by the passing of the car was hot and damp. The afternoon was no better than the forenoon. It was, if anything, worse.

"I could do with a swim," he remarked conversationally.

Abby held the jewel case in both hands. She said, "So could I. Now, to get back to what we were saying –"

He said, "Well, frankly, it's fifty-fifty, as to your first two questions. I *am* mad – which is a masterpiece of understatement – because of you; also, the alliance, viewed impartially, is hardly edifying, but as far as Val is concerned . . . if that's what she wants, more power to her."

"Did you notice," said Abby, "that no one said anything about being deliriously in love?"

"For that you gotta give 'em credit," said Barry. He whistled. "Wait till Mother hears this. She'll want a blow-by-blow description. Val, with a notebook and in battle dress," he went on, "peace, it's wonderful."

They turned into the driveway and he slowed the car. "It just occurs to me," he said, "you've been busy discussing my reactions, what about your own? You're a remarkable girl, Abby."

She said slowly, "I couldn't believe it when Madge and Craig spoke of the possibility. I told you, remember, that I was hurt? I still thought that, when we walked in and found Val practically in possession – and yet when Father made the announcement, I didn't feel anything."

"That's curious," said Barry, with interest. "Why not?"

"I don't know . . . unless it's because it doesn't affect you or me . . . anything that doesn't can't really matter. And yet –"

"Yet what?" he demanded. "Come clean."

"I'm just puzzled," she said. "There's something else, some motive. . . ."

"Well, naturally," he said, "and a child could recognize it . . . even an unmercenary child."

"I don't mean Val."

"Your father? Isn't that just as obvious? You run out on him. He doesn't like it. Val comes up to see the collection – and a fine lot of etchings those turned out to be – and he makes her a nice, respectable proposition. He says, in effect, live with me and be my love . . . it won't be for too long. And frankly," added Barry, and without sparing the blushes, "I would say, not too arduous. This whole maneuver was planned to annoy, distress, and otherwise constriviate you."

"What's that, again?"

197

"It's a good word," Barry defended himself. "Val," he added, "is nothing more than a door, albeit decorative and costly, with which your father can shut you out."

She said, "Maybe . . . but there's more to it than that, I think."

"How much more?"

"I don't know — yet," she admitted.

14

Madge was extremely articulate when, finding her and Duncan at the pool, they broke the news to them. Duncan, who was swimming lazily, went down, and rose gasping with water and laughter. He swung himself up on the ledge and remarked that he had to hand it to Val. Madge, however, was enraged; now that it had actually happened, she could and would not believe it. "Abby, you poor child!" said Madge, half laughing, half crying with genuine indignation.

Abby asked mildly, "Why? I don't mind, Madge . . . it's all right with me. I can even find myself being a little sorry for Val."

"Sorry for Val? Are you out of your mind?" Madge inquired. "She'll do anything she can to get everything she can and to estrange you from your father."

Abby said, "That had reached the saturation point long ago, Madge, even before I was married. There's nothing she can do . . . I'm going to get into my suit and take a swim."

But in the dressing room, she wondered. Was there anything Val could do . . . or her father?

Nothing, as far as logic and reason could determine, yet a nebulous anxiety was a faint mist over her mind. She shook herself mentally to clear it away and presently went back to the pool, where she found Madge characteristically complaining that she and Bob probably wouldn't be asked to the wedding. "And we're family now, for better or worse," she had reminded her listeners.

Barry said lazily, "Sure, when Abby took me on those terms she took you too, but her father didn't."

"Well, just the same," said Madge, "he might ask us. And Val owes us some consideration."

To her amazement Val wrote a graceful little note . . . would Madge and Bob come . . . there wasn't time for formal invitations. She and Norman were being married in the Congregationalist church. Her home, she added, was not geared for even a small reception, as her mother was not well. The reception would be at the Wallace house.

And she telephoned Abby before the weekend was over. She said, "I'll be in town Tuesday . . . could I come in and see you, Abby? I'll be in a welter of course, getting some clothes together. I thought we could talk wedding. Around six, then?"

At six, she arrived, looking cool in black linen with a white blouse. Abby opened the door, Val came in and looked around. She said, "Madge did wonders with a little chintz, didn't she? It looks a different place."

"Different?" asked Abby, before she thought.

"Quite . . . I've been here," she explained casually, "a time or two, in Barry's bachelor days."

She sat down, took off her hat, shook her head at Abby's automatic suggestion of a drink. She said, "I haven't much time . . . I'm meeting some people for dinner . . . a sort of spinster supper." She laughed. "Abby, you're very decent, saying you'll stand up with me. Good Lord, what an expression!"

Abby said only, "I suppose you want to decide on what I'll wear."

"As it isn't a big wedding," said Val, "I'm wearing a suit." She sighed. "It seems too bad, I'd always had such a divine mental picture of myself, white satin, train a mile long, and family lace. Not that we have any lace in the Stanley ménage, beyond a few yards of tatting. However, it can't be helped and would hardly be suitable."

Abby relinquished her own picture of one of

the Botticelli dresses. She offered, "Well, come look for yourself. . . . I hadn't a trousseau," she remarked, as she opened the clothes cupboard doors, "but I've filled in here and there, since."

"I'm so dark," mourned Val; "I wish I were fair." She added, "I found a print at Bergdorf's . . . a pink and black . . . it's rather nice." She added, very quickly, "I could have managed, you know, as I still rate a discount here and there . . . but Norman has been very generous."

She raised her hand, the diamond shone on it, and Abby's eyes followed the shining. Val said, with over deprecation, "What with taxes and all, it was awfully extravagant, but he insisted. I'm to have pearls too," she added, and looked at those which gleamed around Abby's throat.

Abby said, "It's a beautiful ring, Val. Do you see anything here that would do?"

Val plucked various garments from the rods and held them at arms' length. "I have a swatch of the material here," she said, "in my handbag. This aqua print, Abby . . . I think it will look . . ." She laid it over a chair in the bedroom and went to fetch the swatch. "No," she decided. "Do you like the gray? I do."

"The gray" was a short frock, for afternoon, with a square neck and full length sleeves. The color of a dove's breast, it

202

would wash most women out.

Abby said, "I'll try it on . . . and you can see."

She took off her cotton frock, slipped the gray dress over her head, shook out the skirt. Her hair burned above it, and even her pallor triumphed. Val, scowling with concentration, held the little square of pink threaded with spidery black against it. She said, "That does it . . . and you can carry pink flowers if we can find them."

Abby got out of the frock and hung it back in place. Val looked at her, in her scant underthings. She thought, I have never disliked anyone as much, really.

Not that her own figure wasn't superlative, her own skin smooth as cream. . . .

She said, a little harshly, watching Abby put on her dress, run a comb through her hair, "I suppose you think I'm practically beneath contempt."

Abby swung around on the dressing-table bench. The bedroom was a little dark at this time of day, and close. She asked, "Why should I?"

"I don't pretend," said Val, "that I'm in love with your father."

"No. I admire you for it."

Val said, "It would be absurd. It's also the last thing he wants. I respect Norman, I'm fond of him," she went on. It sounded true, and was not. "I'm grateful to him." That was true enough. "As for him," she said, "he isn't in love with me, of course."

Abby smiled faintly, and Val's color rose.

She said furiously, "He could be! It has been known. . . ."

"Of course," said Abby consolingly, "but Father isn't exactly romantic."

Val said sullenly, "It was an arrangement. I amuse him, he likes having me around . . . I'm helpful . . . in his work, in his house . . . I'll make him a good wife, Abby, and a good hostess."

"I'm sure of it," said Abby pleasantly.

Val thought, I could shake her, I could murder her. The violence of her thoughts made her feel unsteady. She rose from the arm of the chair on which she had been sitting and looked around the room. It was quite commonplace, it had little to recommend it. She thought of the room that would be her own at the Wallace house, her house . . . the room that connected with Norman Wallace's through dressing-room doors. . . .

But this room, this inferior little room which Abby shared with Barry Lambert —

She said, "I think I'll take you up on that drink, after all."

She was drinking it when Barry came in. He looked hot, and his red hair was damp and disheveled. He said, "Well, if it isn't my prospective mother-in-law," and grinned. He sank into a chair. "God, what a day ... Abby, I'd take you out to dinner tonight, but I have a meeting ... a few cold meats and a spot of Scotch will do." He regarded Val. "She's getting to be a short-order cook. Val, what brings you to our humble hovel?"

"Clothes."

"If you need any," said Barry, "you can have mine. This instant."

"A fascinating offer," said Val. "I mean, clothes for the wedding."

In pious horror Barry, said, "Is anyone wearing any? Don't tell me you expect me to appear in striped pants!"

"Flannels and a blue coat," said Val.

She set down the empty glass. "I'll have to rush," she said, "if I'm to make my date."

Barry said, "Wait a minute. How's your family taking this?"

"My father doesn't like it. He's very New England, you know, and can't forget that the Wallaces have always been good customers." Her voice was sharp. "Mother's in two minds. She's agreeable to the notion that I've found a good provider, but at the same time a little on the defensive. When it comes to what the neighbors are going to say and think. . . ."

"You can't," said Barry, "blame her *or* the neighbors."

Val bit her lips. She said smoothly, "Aunt Ellen, on the other hand, is in a tizzy. She thinks it beautiful. She's by way of being our local poet, you know. She went so far as to write Norman and tell him that she hoped that the sunset of his life would be brightened by the warm golden sun of my morning-glory youth."

"Good God," said Barry, "I don't believe it! Did she tell you so?"

"Norman showed it to me. He thought it priceless. Also," she went on, "Aunt Ellen said she likewise hoped that his lonely house would be informed by the patter of little feet."

"Words fail me," said Barry piously, "and Abby is likewise speechless and bug-eyed. What did the bridegroom say to that delicate reminder?"

"That it's an idea," answered Val carelessly, and rose, "and one we've talked over. 'Bye, you two. See you at rehearsal Friday night."

She went out and they heard her high heels on the stairs. Barry stared wordlessly at Abby. He asked finally, "Did you hear that?"

She nodded.

"Do you believe it?"

She asked, "Who was it said she believed three impossible things before breakfast?"

"I wouldn't know. And this isn't before breakfast — Abby, it's too absurd."

"I said," she reminded him, "he might have dynastic aspirations . . . a son, for instance." Her voice was edged. "A healthy son."

"Don't look like that, darling."

She said, "Men of his age have children. Val's strong and quite sane."

Barry said, "Come here, Abby." And when she had done so he pulled her into his lap. He said. "That old — "

She put her hand over his mouth. "Never mind the barrack-room description," she said. "Barry, Val will want to make her position secure."

"Oh, sure, he'll have co-operation," said Barry, "and, in one sense, it will be enthusiastic."

Abby said, "It's funny somehow . . . the possibility of a child, and not a grandchild."

"Statistics," said Barry, "are agin it."

Abby rose suddenly. She said, her voice rising, "Barry, why didn't we think of it before?"

"Of what?" he demanded. "A little stepbrother?"

"No. We've been so obsessed with wondering if we could trace Dr. Gilpin's records . . . we don't need them. We need only the man who signed my mother's death certificate. He would know how she died. He would have been a local man."

Barry said, with mounting excitement, "Of course . . . what a dope I am. But who was he, Abby, and is he still there?"

"The local man is a Dr. Lansing . . . but there was someone before him, Barry. In the attic," she said slowly, trying to remember, "there are some books, belonging to my mother . . . I went through them once . . . Mrs. Gambel had put them up there. There were several, poetry, I think . . . with a man's name in them . . . I can't remember the name . . . I remember . . . Fairton . . . and M.D. after the name."

"Who would know?" he asked.

"Anyone who'd lived long enough in Fairton. Dr. Lansing, of course, and possibly Mrs. Gambel," said Abby. "We could ask her, Barry. She came to the house shortly after Mother died. I was a year or so old, I suppose. But she had lived in Fairton before she came there as housekeeper to the Greenways."

"Has Mrs. Gambel a phone?" asked Barry. "Or if not, has she a neighbor with one. You could talk to the operator, ask to have her call you back, tonight, if you can't reach her directly. Get busy . . . I'll wash and change."

She said, "But dinner . . . and your meeting?"

"This can't wait. We'll get something around the corner, or go without till later. Get on that phone."

Abby went to the telephone, took it from its cradle, and asked, "May I have information, please?"

15

The afternoon of the wedding was cooler, for which the guests gave thanks. The Stanleys sat in a front pew, Val's mother, her father's sister Ellen, her father's brother Saul and his wife. Across from them Madge sat between her husband and Barry. She wore subdued, sheer black but a fantastic hat. After the ceremony Robert Duncan complained that his shins were black and blue and his ribs bruised.

Mr. Stanley gave his daughter away. He was a hard, brown, elderly man, with great integral dignity. Her mother, watching, was almost expressionless. Val, thought Madge, had done well by Mrs. Stanley. Her frock was lovely, and her big brimmed hat. She had been a very handsome woman before she had lost weight, as her health had failed.

Aunt Ellen was the only one who wept. Val's uncle looked as if he cheered. He was, after all, a real estate agent, and Wallace, he reflected, would have friends ... Val would see to that. His wife also looked happy. She was wondering how many Fairton women she would ask to the tea she planned for Val ... Val couldn't say no, or could she?

Madge nudged Bob. "I have never before seen Ellen Stanley in anything but amorphous foulards," she whispered.

Barry looked at Abby. Her frock was a gray cloud, her pale-pink hat, a halo. She carried roses, shading from flesh to deep pink ... and her face was like a rose, roused from its pallor. She wore her mother's carved pink corals, in her ears and around her wrists and throat.

He deliberately did not look at Val. She made his gorge rise, standing beside the tall old man with the unrevealing face. Craig Emerson was Wallace's best man. He looked ill, and might well have been. Last night after rehearsal he had drunk too much.

The clergyman was a newcomer to Fairton. He had liked his new parish or had until now. He did not like officiating at this wedding, but he had his duty to perform to his parishioners.

The organist crashed into the usual happy-ending music. He was feeling a little sardonic. He was a local young man, who had come home not long ago with an honorable discharge from

the navy, to his wife and child. He had known
Val Stanley since she was in pig-tails and, at one
time, rather well . . . until she decided that
Fairton was not her appropriate setting. Well,
she had returned to it. . . .

Val's parents appeared at the Wallace house
and partook sparingly of what the Fairton
weekly would refer to as the "collation." They
left early, as Mrs. Stanley, her husband explained, was not equal to too much excitement.
Aunt Ellen remained until the last decent moment. She had never set foot in this house before . . . and, if she knew Val, she wouldn't
again, or at least not often. She might be the local poet, but she was also New England and,
aside from her pangs of creation, realistic. Craig
Emerson, who had felt terrible for a week, sick
with nerves and anger, was sorry for her. She
was having such a good time, her thin cheeks
flushed and her high voice higher after two
glasses of excellent champagne. He saw her
look wistfully around the drawing room, so seldom used, and asked her quietly if she would
like to see some of the collection.

Jay Morris was circulating among the guests.
He had been a fascinated spectator at the
wedding. It could not affect him — he was necessary to the collection.

He talked, for the most part, to Madge, whom

he found immensely entertaining. But he watched Abby. He thought, She's the loveliest thing in this house, and sighed because she had left it.

As for Val, he thought less than nothing of her. Craig had tried to draw him out, but Morris had little to say, not from loyalty but from sheer indifference. He had said, merely, after he had been informed of the plans:

"What difference does it make? If she wants the Wallace money — or as much of it as he will leave her — she will have earned it, provided she sticks it out. Why so distressed, Craig? It's nothing to either of us."

And of Val, he said, "Her looks won't last . . . her bones aren't good. Give her twenty years, or less, and she'll coarsen. But by that time it won't matter to Norman."

Now, Barry wandered up to his wife, a glass in his hand. He asked, "Didn't I do a good job of kissing the bride?"

"Too good," she said, laughing. She didn't care tonight. She was too happy, too irradiated with happiness.

He said low, "They'll be going soon . . . have you told him?"

"I haven't had an opportunity."

"Want me to?"

"No," she said; "this is between us."

The opportunity came later, when she saw her father turn away from Saul Stanley and join Val. She went to him, smiled at Val. She said, "You'll be leaving soon."

They were driving ... staying overnight in Massachusetts en route to Maine. No one had inquired where the gas came from.

Wallace looked at his watch and nodded, and Val said, "I'll go up and change. I won't be long. Come along, Abby."

That was routine, of course; the matron of honor assisting the bride. Abby said, "In a moment."

Val went to the stairs, and people clustered there, waiting. She threw her flowers, orchids, white, pink, pale green, in the customary gesture. Aunt Ellen, back from her brief tour, caught them ... there was no one else to catch them, except Abby or Madge, or Saul Stanley's wife.

"I wanted them," Madge said sadly to her husband.

"My child," he said firmly, "haven't you been married enough?"

"I hope so —" she looked a little dreamy — "but every time I go to a wedding I have, you might say, the urge."

He said kindly, "If it lasts until we get home I shall be gratified to beat it out of you."

She took his arm, smiling. She wasn't at all romantic about Bob any more . . . but he was quite necessary to her. She thought, watching Val disappear up the curving stairs, Good Lord, I wonder if I've really settled down? Aloud she inquired, "Where's Abby? She should be trailing up after Val."

"I saw her a moment ago," said Bob, "with her father."

"Oh, murder!" said Madge hopefully. "Do you suppose she's telling him what she thinks of him, or just wishing him luck?"

"If the latter," said Bob, "he'll need it."

Abby and her father were in the small reception room, and the door was closed. She had closed it. Over the mantel, where her mother's portrait had looked down, another painting hung . . . in remembrance . . . one of the small Botticellis.

Her father said, with comprehensible impatience, "Well, Abby, you wished to speak with me?"

She had been looking at the Botticelli, thinking of the portrait. They would hang it, she and Barry, as soon as they returned to town.

She looked gravely at her father. She said, "It won't take long. I just wanted to tell you that Barry and I have been to see Dr. Mason."

"Dr. Mason?" he frowned slightly. "But who,"

he inquired "is he? and why should it —"

She said, "Surely you remember him, Father? He was the local man before Dr. Lansing."

His face was very controlled. He had recognized Mason's name at once, she thought.

"Well?" he said, with exaggerated patience. "I must remind you, Abby, that Valentine and I —"

She said, "Dr. Mason is practicing in New Jersey. He was quite young when he was here, and unmarried. It was in fact at your suggestion that he left Fairton."

"My suggestion?"

She said, "He's not young now, and he's happily married, and he didn't mind talking about it. He attended my mother several times. He was impressionable and he told us she was the most beautiful and the most unhappy creature he had ever seen. He was in love with her, and she, with him."

Wallace's face darkened. He said, with cold fury, "What indecent nonsense. . . ."

"She used to meet him," said Abby softly, "when she went walking . . . she'd wait, and he'd stop, on his way back from a call. It was all very innocent," she added, "which was a pity."

"Abby, I forbid you!"

She said, "On one of those walks she caught

216

cold. It rained, very suddenly and hard, and she waited in the rain. He didn't come . . . there had been an emergency. So he always blamed himself, because she caught cold, and it became pneumonia and she died of it. You *had* to call him, father. You tried getting a man from New York, and others from nearer by . . . but they couldn't come at once and it had by then become immediate. He didn't dare move her to the hospital. Everything possible was done, but she died, and he was with her. You weren't. You found dying distasteful, I dare say."

He said, "The man's a fool and a liar as well."

"No," Abby interrupted. "He isn't. I was glad he told us. She had a little happiness, after all, even if it was frightened and incomplete. And she died," said Abby softly, "in her right mind and of pneumonia. It is in the records."

He said heavily, "Are you so sure? Mason was a man you could bribe. . . ."

"No," said Abby. "My mother was never insane, not even temporarily, as you suggested, nor when I was born. She may have looked as she did, and as I now look, but she was strong, and healthy. She was unhappy but never neurotic. Dr. Mason had some letters from her. He had kept them. He showed them to us. He said he went to see her parents later. For a long time he grieved, very much. He felt that he had killed her . . . that if he had not kept her waiting there in the autumn rain. . . .''

But Wallace was walking past her, he had opened the door and gone.

She followed him, and went upstairs, the back way. Val had changed to a dark shantung suit, with an absurd and becoming hat. She wore alligator wedgies and her big alligator handbag lay near by. She turned from the mirror and asked, "What happened to you?"

"I was talking to Father," said Abby. "And you didn't need me."

"Mrs. Renning came in," said Val, "and Morton has taken the luggage."

This was Val's room. She had moved into it, as far as personal belongings were concerned, before her marriage. She looked around it, a moment. She asked, "What were you and Norman talking about . . . me?"

"No."

Uneasiness crept over Val. She picked up the handbag . . . it was very beautiful. The pearls shone around her throat and the diamond was bright on her finger, above the wedding ring. She said, "Well, I'm ready."

Abby opened the door and stood aside. She said, "I hope you will be as happy as I am, Val."

Val's face flushed carnation red.

She said, "Thanks, darling," lightly and thought, as she went slowly downstairs where the guests and Norman Wallace waited, I'll pay her back for that, if it's the last thing I ever do.

16

The return of the Norman Wallaces to Fairton inaugurated a new social era. For the first time in the memory of the amazed inhabitants the Wallace house became almost as populous as Grand Central Terminal . . . emerging, in one unheralded, blinding glare, from the dim-out of the last twenty-odd years. Before his marriage to Abby's mother, Wallace, when in residence, had been definitely inhospitable and his home was open only to those people whose interest in the collection, whether professional or informed amateur, gave them a priority. After his first marriage, he exhibited his wife at a brief series of stately gatherings and then, following her death, reverted to his isolationist attitude. But apparently Val, having acquired the keys of the household, had converted him to a startling geniality.

At least, it made for conversation, at Red Cross after church, over picket fences, in autumnal gardens, and at the Sewing Circle, or the markets. People compared notes. "Were you invited?" they asked, and, "Have you seen the paper?" Everyone had seen the local paper, which announced soberly that the Wallace collection would now be open to the general public on the last Thursday of each month from two to six, with Mr. Craig Emerson acting in capacity of guide and expert.

Then there were the social gatherings almost as soon as the bride and bridegroom came home: several teas; a series of small dinners; a cocktail party. The town was agog and had more to talk about than anything else since Pearl Harbor, except the war and Val Stanley's marriage.

Val was too socially wise to make definite first- and second-string demarcations. She mixed her people as expertly as she mixed a drink. Even Aunt Ellen was included, and so deftly that it was always a day or two thereafter before Aunt Ellen realized that "tea at my niece's" was exactly the same, save for the setting, as teas at the home of any member of the Fairton Reading Society . . . in as far as her fellow tea drinkers were concerned.

Nor was Fairton the only town to be given the adrenalin of an increased social tempo; people in neighboring villages, who knew Wallace slightly, or Val rather better, also were bidden and came. And from New York there came, with growing frequency, still other visitors, for a day, an evening, or even a weekend . . . and, as Madge Duncan remarked to her husband, "*such* people . . . anything from the social register to . . ." she paused and added delicately, "the Kennel Club, Darling, *did* you see that wall-eyed blonde with the jade anklet Val had with her in the village yesterday?"

Val's friends, fabulous young women walking like Powers goddesses; equally fabulous young men, in and out of uniform . . . infant colonels in the Air Corps, on leave; scrubbed, immaculate majors, whose wonderful pinks obscured the fact that they were calloused from sitting on desk chairs and on lids; willowy civilians of both sexes who decorated or designed . . . a sprinkling of promising writers (male) and those who did more than promise (female) — exciting refugees with authentic or ersatz titles . . . young actresses and bit screen players; a musician or two . . .

Also Norman Wallace's friends or acquaintances . . . men interested in art, commercially or otherwise, fellow members of the clubs he never set foot in; and very often, their wives; men with a background of Who's Who and Bradstreet. It was all very confusing.

Madge and Robert Duncan were meticulously asked to all the larger gatherings and a few of the small; and so were Abby and Barry.

Abby cried, reading one of Val's notes over the breakfast table, "But what does it *mean?*"

Weekends, going up to Madge's, they had also found themselves at the Wallaces. "Do go, angels," Madge would urge, "it's too astonishing, a liberal education; besides, you'll be amused."

Abby wasn't but Barry was . . . he found it excellent entertainment; Val's public attitude toward Abby was a minor miracle . . . a warm kindliness, as befitted a stepmother; a species of understanding, linked-arms camaraderie, as befitted their contemporary ages . . . plus a rather charming depreciation, which you couldn't quite pin down — almost an apology for being there, presiding in Abby's place.

Now, Abby gave him Val's letter. It was written on the heavy creamy paper she affected, monogrammed, with the engraved address — "do hope you can make it . . . just a small party," wrote Val. "Saturday evening . . . Why don't you come to us for the weekend, if you haven't already promised Madge? We'd love to have you. . . ."

"Let's go," said Barry, deciding suddenly.

She said, "But —"

"Look Mrs. Lambert. Val's playing some sort

223

of parlor, bedroom and bath game. I'd like to figure it out. Wouldn't you?"

She said, "It's so utterly unlike Father. He despises most people . . . and he's never liked young people. First thing you know, she'll have a swimming pool, tennis courts, badminton . . . all the things he hates."

Barry asked shrewdly, "Aren't you feeling a little sorry for him?"

She said slowly, "No, I don't think so."

"Watch it," he warned her; "perhaps that's just exactly what he wants you to feel."

"But why?" she demanded. "It doesn't make sense."

He said persuasively, "Just the same, let's go . . . innocent bystanders, spectators. October's a good month up there . . . and you rate a little fun. You've been very much neglected lately."

It was true enough. In September, Barry had begun his night school law course. On the evenings when he was not at the university, he was doing pre-election work in the district. Abby was alone a good deal. Later, of course, Madge would be back in town and would offer her house, her friends, her general aura of active excitement, if Abby wished to take advantage of these. Now and then, a school friend turned up, and telephoned her. She was herself taking a course, in Nurse's Aide, and at its completion would give a stated number of hours to the hospital. But the fact remained that no matter how she occupied her time, it was still empty, if Barry was not with her.

She was, of course, going to have a baby. Not now, not yet, but sometime. There was no reason why she shouldn't have one . . . no problem of war, postwar, economics; no problem of heredity.

She said suddenly, "Suppose Val's started a baby?"

Barry shook his red head. "Nope," he said, "Haven't we been over all that before? Afraid she'll beat you to it?" He smiled at her across the little table. "Darling, there's time, all the time in the world. Let's go up for the weekend. I can't get away until Saturday morning and I'll have to come down Sunday night. But you can go Friday. . . ."

"Not without you."

He said, "What are you scared of, Abby? Okay, Saturday then. Call Val and insist upon the red carpet and the fatted — it will probably be duck. Tell her I know where I can find a carton of cigarettes and a bottle of Scotch without resorting to the black markets. That will make us doubly welcome. And take a tape measure with you," he suggested, "and, when she isn't looking —"

"Barry!"

He said, "Well, ask her outright then!"

Val met them, with Craig and a number of parcels in the back seat. She was looking very well, tanned and glowing. She had put on a little weight, which became her. Her face was as smooth as nature and sun-bronzed pancake could made it, and as guileless as a good child's. Her dark head was bare, her suit was a soft monotone tweed, her hand-knit sweater a wonderful orange gold.

Craig looked bad, but his face lighted a little when he saw Abby. At Val's gesture, Abby got in the back seat with him and Barry in the front. Val said expansively, "I've been doing the marketing . . . it becomes more and more difficult. Mrs. Renning, capable as she is, simply cannot cope . . . and ordering by phone is half as satisfactory and twice as expensive."

Craig spoke low, and bitterly. "The perfect wife," he said.

Abby asked, "What in the world are they doing to the Corner Market?"

It was so obvious that they were painting it that no one answered. But she would not let herself be drawn into a discussion of Val and Craig.

Val spoke, over her shoulder, "The town's getting itself a new hair-do . . . Father's busier than he's been in years," she said.

Barry said something about labor and materials, and Val shrugged. She said, "Some of the Fairton men are home, discharged from the services. There's enough to keep them busy. I persuaded Norman to put another man in the garden. After all, Morton's too used to having his own way and too damned lazy," she added with energy, "for his way to be much good. After the war," she went on, turning into the road that led to the house, "Norman thinks we can build a swimming pool . . . if the cost isn't too out of this world. I was talking to Madge about it the other day. Of course, she didn't build theirs, it was already on the place, but she had to have repairs down and she knows a firm that specializes. . . ."

Barry cleared his throat with such vigor that the rest of the sentence was lost to Abby. She had an impulse to laugh aloud. "Swimming pool, tennis courts, badminton," she had said to Barry only a few days ago. She had been a better prophet than she realized.

Each time she had seen her father since his wedding she had looked for some alteration in him to match the alteration in his manner of living. Yet he seemed the same, gray and unrevealing; no older, no younger. His manner toward her had not changed, it was the same he had always employed – in public. He avoided being alone with her. Not that she wished to be alone with him . . . yet, there was, as Barry had said the night of the wedding, plenty of unfinished business. Wallace had neither explained his falsification of the facts in her mother's death nor denied that he had falsified them. He had simply walked out of the room the night of the wedding and, metaphorically, never returned.

His manner toward Val was noteworthy. He behaved toward his wife, Abby realized, as he had never behaved toward her . . . as if Val were an indulged, beloved and devoted daughter. He was never, at least when they were on exhibition, disciplinary or ironic with her. He watched her quietly, often smiling a little. He seemed proud of her, of the way, as he once expressed it, in which she had "taken hold."

Toward their guests he was a considerate host, if an unbending one. He made no attempt to join them in the various activities at which they were amateurs or experts; he did not drink more than his abstemious custom. He never played cards; he watched while the others rolled up the rugs and danced. If there was too much radio, too loud laughter, too much anything, he vanished quietly and without ostentation, and reappeared when it suited him. If, as Barry suggested when he and Abby were alone in the room that had once been hers, the new life was getting Wallace down, he did not show it.

Toward Barry he was amiable, and showed not the slightest trace of his old hostility. But Barry said, as he and Abby were dressing for dinner. "You know, don't you, that your old man hates my guts? What bothers me is why he no longer troubles to show it."

Abby was brushing her hair. The blue October dusk crowded against the windows and a small wind spoke of snow on distant mountains. In Abby's big room a fire burned on the little hearth, and its dancing light was on her hair.

A peaceful room . . . many windowed. The great bed in which she had slept since childhood was gone and twin beds took its place. There were fresh curtains at the windows, a new dressing-table bench, an unfamiliar chair. It had become a guest room. There were late-blooming chrysanthemums in low vases, small massed flowers, soft bronze and dusky pink, pale yellow. . . .

Barry stood by the fireplace and watched his wife . . . the brush went crackling through her hair . . . lifted it, smoothed it, the satin length, the incredible color. He thought he would never tire of watching her.

She said, "I don't understand my father."

Her glance, as she turned, went to her desk. It was one she had liked very much, and once it had been untidy, cluttered with letters, with calendars and scratch pads. It was neat now, green blottered with Val's stationery in silver racks, there were assorted pens and pencils, a silver inkwell and — final gesture of the perfect hostess, books of stamps, three-, six- and eight-cent.

He said, "Try not to care. You're so edgy with him, Abby. And you shy away from Val like a nervous horse."

It was not the most fortunate of similes and it irritated her, unduly. She put down the brush and began to braid her hair. She would wear it that way tonight, wrapped around and around her head. She would wear the thin wool dress Barry particularly liked, very sheer wool, and almost the color of her eyes.

He asked, "Have I ever told you how pretty you are? Only that isn't the adequate word."

She said, "You just said I was like a horse."

"Nothing's prettier than a horse," he assured her, and came over to bend down, put his cheek against her hair. He said, "Don't be afraid of Val."

"I'm not. Why should I be?"

"God knows. Abby, you and I — are together. We belong. We knew that the day we met . . . a

230

moment, an eternity ago, when was it . . . last May? What your father does, or what Val does, that needn't concern us. On the surface it simply looks as if she were spending all the money she can lay her hands on, and as fast as possible. Personally I don't think that's too bright, but it's quite possible that he has told her that after his death she'll have her dower right and no more. On the other hand, I believe there's something underneath the more or less to be expected gestures . . . I don't know whether it's of Val's motivation or whether it's your father's; or whether, whatever it is, they dreamed it up together . . . but it's there. And I'm just curious enough to want to know what it is and why."

Abby pinned the braids in place with steady fingers. She asked, "Where did you and Val disappear to, just before we came upstairs?"

"Disappear?" He looked at her blankly. "Oh, that . . . Your father wanted an expert opinion on the brandy somebody sold him last week. Val took me down to the cellar. It's quite a setup. For a man who doesn't drink seriously, he certainly laid in a stock of the nasty stuff, over a long period of time. And hate me or not, he must trust me, not only," said Barry, grinning, "with his beautiful bride but with the keys to his liquor closets."

Abby made no comment. There wasn't one to

make. Barry went off to the bathroom, whistling. He thought, Whatever the old man's game, Val's is obvious enough. A man. Any man . . . in of course a totally harmless and discreet way . . . at least for the moment.

She had said, standing there in the whitewashed cellars, with the lights too bright overhead; "I don't suppose you'll believe I'm really happy?"

"Why not?" he told her. "You have everything all clever girls work hard to get — "

She said, "I don't mind your saying that, because it's true. And I am happy. Barry, have you forgotten what I said to you . . . the day you and I were in the sun porch, just before Norman announced our engagement?"

"Yes," he said promptly.

She smiled, took his arm, and moved closer to him. She still wore the same scent. He remembered it. You always remember scents. She said, "Good. Because if you'd said you remembered, I was going to ask you to forget."

Nuts, he thought now and looked at himself in the mirror. He looked a little fine drawn for him. It wasn't easy to return to the classroom and to books, he had been out of that sort of thing for a long time . . . but he liked it fine. He liked tearing around with Hageney; he liked smoky little clubrooms and bigger, better aired clubrooms. He liked people . . . all kinds of people. He talked with them, on subways, in buses . . . at bars. This was merely a very small beginning, but one day it would pay off. A lot of people in his district had sons in the services, some would return. They were wondering what would happen when they did. They were wondering about their sons' desire for further education, or their chances for jobs . . . reconversion couldn't absorb them all, they argued; there would be a transition period; and it would be bad. One man had said, "Lambert, I've got two kids in the Air Corps. One of them had never done a day's work, he was just out of school, see. The other had a twenty-dollar-a-week job. Now they're earning a hell of a lot of money, by comparison. When they come back they'll have to take — if anything — what will look like chicken feed to them. There'll be too many of them for the commercial airlines to place. Sure, there'll be airplane factories but any god's quantity of trained mechanics . . . too many to fit into all the factories, all the machine shops. So what? Lambert, you tell me. . . ."

"Barry, for heaven's sake," said Abby. "What are you doing?"

He said, "Darling, I'm standing here looking in the mirror marveling how anyone as beautiful as I wasn't snapped up by the cinema long ago."

She said, "I've wondered too . . . but do get dressed. The gong rang just now."

"Now we have gongs," said Barry. That entertained him, too . . . a little trick Val must have picked up through lending library association with the stately homes of England. A dressing gong; a warning or cocktail gong; a dinner gong. He thought, Hail, hail, the gongs all here. . . .

"Coming, mother," he said meekly.

17

Before they left Sunday evening, Wallace took Barry into his library. He said, "Sit down, Barry, I want to talk to you."

He pushed an inlaid-silver cigarette box across the desk and regarded his son-in-law. He said, "I think I owe you an apology."

"Why?" asked Barry warily.

Wallace said thoughtfully, "On the other hand, I doubt if any sane man could contemplate calmly so hasty a marriage as yours and Abby's. So I don't owe you an apology for my original objection ... But I would like to say that I have revised my opinion of you. I have made —" he paused slightly — "inquiries. It seems that you are serious about a career in politics."

Barry said hastily, "I'd hardly call it that, sir."

"Well, whatever you call it ... it is," he added, "in its way quite admirable, although I belong to the reactionary school, which holds that gentlemen are rarely politicians or, shall we say, the other way around?"

Barry said, annoyed, "I'm afraid I can't agree with you. It depends of course on what your definition of a gentleman is. But by any standards, I could cite some notable names."

Wallace smiled. He said, "Suppose we don't argue the point. I personally do not belong to any party, and upon the occasions when I have voted I have exercised the right of choice."

"Fair enough," said Barry, wondering how Wallace managed to keep an apparently inexhaustible supply of his custom-made, rather heavy cigarettes.

"When I have given funds," said Wallace, "to either party it has been because at the time, I preferred one to the other. From all your mother tells me —" he stopped and added mildly — "she is a very articulate woman — your particular interest lies in reform . . . and your party affiliation is more or less a matter of convenience. In other words, you have to work through or with an organization machine."

Barry raised his eyebrows. "You put it," he murmured, "neatly."

"I'm not interested," said Wallace, "in reform. I've lived long enough to see reformers fail, too often, and people revert to type — to greed, stultifying stupidity, and self-destruction despite all the brave words. I don't especially like the world I live in but as it's the only one of which I have actual knowledge I have had to adapt myself, after my fashion." He opened the desk drawer with a small key and took out an envelope. "I did not give you a wedding present," he said.

"You gave Abby a portrait, Mr. Wallace, and her mother's jewels."

Wallace said, "This, however, is for you . . . to use as you see fit, in furthering your – ambitions."

Barry took the envelope and removed a check. It was sizable, worthy of respect or suspicion, depending on how you look at these things. He said, "This is more than generous. But I would prefer you made the contribution through your state or county chairman."

"It is not a contribution to a party," said Wallace, "it is for you to use, as I said before."

"You mean," asked Barry curiously, "that if I refuse, you wouldn't give it to the Finance Committee here?"

"Just that."

Barry put the check in the envelope and the envelope in his pocket. He thought, Hell, a bribe. But what for, and why? They could use it. Hageney would jump out of his withered skin. His was not a rich district, nor fashionable.

He said, "I'll take it, then. Thanks very much."

Wallace said, "Perhaps it is just my way of admitting I was mistaken . . . I believe you are making Abby very happy."

Barry said bluntly, "She would be — if not happier, at least less bewildered, if she knew why you had told her that her mother was insane, and had committed suicide."

Wallace said regretfully, "I didn't say exactly that . . . she drew her own inferences."

Barry said, "You're damned right she did, as you intended her to. Would you tell me why?"

Wallace considered. Then he said, "Of course. It is simple enough. I did not want her to marry you, and was certain that there was no other way to stop her."

"So you lied?"

"Not to put too fine a point on it, yes. It is true enough that Abby's mother was — neurotic." He looked at Barry levelly. "But only because she was unhappy. As you were with Abby when she saw Dr. Mason, you know that . . . She was not unhappy early in our marriage. She was quite content, with as much as I could give her. Later I was apparently unable to give her enough. She was a very intelligent young woman. She wished to leave me, but circumstances prevented that. After Abby was born she fancied herself in love with Mason. I knew it, naturally. I watched her change. I saw her color, when the telephone rang or the mail was delivered . . . I watched her go off on the ostensibly solitary excursions. It seemed harmless enough, and it diverted her. To some extent it also diverted me, and relieved me of the somewhat oppressive affection she had centered on me before Abby's birth."

Barry said, "You're incredible, as I suppose you know."

"To you, yes." He rose. "I hope you and Abby will come here often. It is pleasant for me to have you here, and for Valentine. You have been wondering," he remarked leaning against the desk, "while I was talking. You have been thinking that in middle life I made a failure of a marriage to a woman greatly my junior; and that now, practically moribund, I am repeating that error. But I do not think so. Valentine is very dissimilar from my first wife. She is extremely intelligent, in her way, and realistic. She is quite aware of her bargain."

He walked to the door and opened it and Barry followed. He thought, What a — swine. The expression "independent as a hog on ice" occurred to him. It was a silly colloquialism and he had never been sure what it meant but it suited his father-in-law.

The check burned in his pocket. In the train, he told Abby exactly what her father had said. She listened without comment, and he asked anxiously, "I shouldn't have taken it, should I?"

"Why not?" asked Abby. "If it's his way of making amends. It isn't a very good way, but you can make it so."

"The end, if not the means?" He smiled at her. "But I don't think that was his motive. He is trying either to buy me or disarm me. I don't know which. And certainly he was frank enough about the whole situation."

She said, "That would disarm you too. Did it?"

"Hell, no. When I think of what he tried to do to you — to us. . . ."

She said, "Let's not talk about it any more." She put her hand in his. "He can't hurt us now."

As the train rocked through the autumnal country, the smell of wood smoke beyond its windows, the trees now in darkness which, by daylight, burned, he said abstractedly, "Abby, it wasn't just that he didn't want you to marry me. He didn't want you to marry anyone . . . not even Emerson."

She roused herself from a little dream, in which she had dismissed her father, everyone, and locked herself and Barry into it as if it were a room. She said, "He wouldn't have minded Craig – much."

"I'm not so sure," said Barry. "Well, skip it. From now on in he'll have his hands full with Val, or I'm not so sharp as I used to be."

"Why?"

"Maybe not now," he said; "she's a smart little dish. But later. You don't think she's going to be content with the sort of admiration he gives a painting? and a minor painting at that, I dare say."

Abby said, "He doesn't seem to mind other people admiring her . . . her friends, I mean. At least he doesn't show it."

Barry grinned, "Tramping through the gallery," he said, "drinking his liquor, making passes at his wife?"

"Well, not actually," Abby argued.

"Val's more attractive to most of her male acquaintances," said Barry, "now that she's married. Safer, more fun, no strings. Now that she is not only married, but has money and a husband who, in their brutal estimate of value given and received, couldn't possibly rate. Give her a couple of years, and I don't think your father will be as happy about the whole thing.

Not that she won't be discreet. . . ."

Abby said, "You know a lot about Val, don't you?"

He said, "Not very much. I used to wonder . . . she has a pretty warm exterior. You ask yourself, What's cookin'? and you think you know. Yet, I've never been sure."

He laughed. He added, "And won't be, now."

Abby looked at him thoughtfully. The car was crowded, but they might have been alone in it. She asked, "You aren't wishing you could find out, by any chance?"

He said, "Nope. I have enough trouble with you. You see," he said, smiling, "about you – I *am* sure."

He watched her color rise, and laughed again. He was a happy man, in a train taking him back to work and his own place, with his wife beside him. He looked forward to the pattern of his life. After election the pace might slacken, but he still had his job to do, his studies and his friends. He thought, without regret, I don't suppose we will be going to Fairton much, this winter. . . .

He was mistaken. Madge and Duncan came to town and opened the apartment. There were parties, theaters, the usual round when Barry was free. Abby completed her Nurse's Aide course and worked at the hospital the nights

Barry was at the university. But they often went to Fairton for a winter weekend. They drifted into it . . . an urgent note from Val, a telephone call, or she might appear at the flat without warning. She'd corralled a general, or it might be a rear admiral, she had the most interesting member of an underground, coming for a weekend, strictly incognito, of course. They must come.

So they went, and the country was clean with snow, pure on the mountains and the rolling foothills and the trees, and almost before they knew it they would be there again. Fewer of Val's former friends appeared, and in their places notable people with stability and substance.

If Abby protested, Barry would say, "But you have to get out, and see people, darling; you can't stay cooped up here all the time."

So she stopped protesting. She told herself, it was people he liked, all kinds of people. He had immense fun on the weekends, arguing, listening, talking. He attracted all types, with his warmth and vitality and talent for friendliness. And Val said seriously, "It's good for him. Abby, the more influential people he knows, the better."

She had to admit that, hating, however, to hear it from Val.

But it wasn't until early spring, until she and Barry had been married almost a year, until people were beginning to look toward Europe with hope in their prayers, that she realized she was deeply, starkly afraid of her father's wife.

18

March was an absurd month; March was warm. March ran a temperature and people dragged off their coats, put away umbrellas, and looked fagged and irritated. In the country, the grass grew green and high, flowering shrubs burst into premature bloom, and the birds came winging back.

Madge left town and took Duncan with her. He complained mildly that Fifth and Park were just beginning to be fit to walk upon again and he had spent hours practicing a long, low whistle. But Madge said firmly that he could whistle in Hot Springs. She had been feeling rheumatic, she told Barry and Abby when, the night before her departure, they dined with her. She wasn't opening the Fairton place for summer until the end of May. She had refused to consider the winter in Florida for reasons both personal and patriotic. But now a spot of Hot Springs was indicated. "Besides," she added, "we might as well be there for all we see of you . . . you hardly ever come up here, Abby, and weekends you are too busy being the devoted daughter."

Abby said, "Barry likes going up — there's always something going on."

Later, Madge swept Abby into her bedroom and ordered, "Powder your nose!"

"It doesn't need it."

"Powder it just the same." Madge sat sideways on a chair, put her arms across the top, and her small brown face was troubled. She said, "Your father, Val, or both, are corrupting Barry, in a minor way."

Abby's eyes widened. She repeated, "Corrupting?"

"All those fantastic people, all that attention —" Madge made a gesture —"it can't be good for him."

Abby said defensively, "He isn't neglecting his work."

"Or you?"

"Of course not. I expected to be alone a good deal when he started to study law, and although he's less active in this district than before election, he still attends meetings."

Madge said, "I am very fond of you, and know better than to stick my neck out, but someone saw Barry lunching in town with Val

246

last week and took pains to tell me about it."

Abby's face was pink. She asked, "Why shouldn't he lunch with her?"

"An admirable attitude," agreed Madge, sweeping a lipstick expertly over her mouth, "but did you know about it?"

"Naturally."

"Then," said Madge, "I've been in a needless tizzy. But just the same, watch yourself. That girl is poison."

When they were home, Abby said, as quietly as she could, "You didn't tell me you lunched with Val last week."

"Who did?" demanded Barry, prowling around the icebox. "Madge's food is good," he said parenthetically, "but not particularly filling; too much on the soufflé side."

Abby was considerably taken aback. She said, "Someone saw you and told Madge."

"The grapevine," said Barry. He found a hunk of ancient, rationed cheese, a bottle of beer and crackers, and sat down at the table. "Join me, Mrs. Lambert?"

She shook her shining head. "Barry, why did you?" she asked.

He looked at her a moment, his black eyes thoughtful. He said, "So I'm to account for myself."

"No. But Val —" She sat down on a straight

247

chair — "and you didn't tell me. I told Madge you did."

"Darling," he said tolerantly, "I know my way around, even with Val. We have an anniversary coming up. I spoke of it to Val the last time we were there. She asked, what was I going to give you? I said, God knows. She said she'd happened to see something that looked like you . . . I said, Okay, lead me to it. We made a date; and she did. She has good taste."

"You have, too," said Abby gravely; "and your mother."

Barry moved his shoulders impatiently. "Don't," he suggested, "be a dope. Incidentally, the project had your respected parent's blessing. He knew about it. It wasn't a secret — except from you."

Abby said stubbornly, "Val could have told you where the shop was — she didn't have to tag along."

"Maybe not, but I'm lost in the mazes of an antique shop, and a poor bargainer. Val's competent. So I sez to her, 'I'll buy you lunch and you'll take me shopping and if you tell Abby I'll cut your lovely white throat.' But now you know, and that," Barry added, "is irritating. Sorry?"

"No," said Abby. She got up. "I don't see any excuse, really."

"Why in hell must I have one?" Barry demanded, suddenly angry. "We go up to Val's house weekends and eat her food and. . . ."

"My father's house, and his food," Abby corrected him.

"She's his wife," said Barry reasonably. "So I still can't see why you are promoting a scene because I take her to lunch!"

"I'm not," said Abby, "you are. After all you've said —"

"Such as —"

"You don't trust her," repeated Abby; "you believe she's up to something; you want to find out what it is —"

"I'll never find out," said Barry, "by remote control." He rose and pushed his chair back, hard. He said, "Did you never have lunch with someone you didn't trust?"

"Often, when we go up to Fairton. By the way, it's you who insist on going, not I; I wouldn't care if I never saw the place again."

Barry said, "I enjoy it. Val has a gift of stage-managing good weekends."

Abby said, "You've always liked her."

"Sure. I think she's a bitch. I thought so before she married your father and I've seen no reason to change my mind since. But that doesn't prevent me from liking her. Why should it? You're being childish."

Abby went out of the little kitchen and into the bedroom. The incredible heat evaporated at night. It was chilly now, and damp. She shivered and the tears were thick in her throat. After a little while, Barry followed here. He pulled her to him, roughly. He said, "Abby, do grow up."

"Because I don't like you lunching with Val — that's not adult?" she inquired, stifled.

He laughed, and his anger was gone. "Perhaps it isn't. On the other hand, it's flattering." He kissed her. He said, "It was fun, rather. Val complained a little of her role as old man's darling, in an oblique sort of way. I didn't rise to it. I won't say I wouldn't be interested in details, but I thought, better not. Then she tried to find out from me if you were in an interesting condition. Said she thought you looked pale and drawn last weekend. I told her that we were planning twins, boy and girl, yellow hair, black eyes . . . but hadn't set the date, merely the specifications. She looked relieved."

Abby said, pulling herself away, "I'd just as soon you didn't discuss me with Val."

"Darling, I don't; she does. Get your silly clothes off and come to bed. Next time I go shopping for a gift for you I'll go alone and return with a monstrosity for which I have paid too much. Like that better?"

"Much."

Later, when he was nearly asleep, she spoke to him. "Barry," she asked, "are you awake?"

"I am now, worse luck. What is it, for Pete's sake?"

"Just – did you buy whatever it was Val selected?"

"Nope."

"Why not?"

"She was wrong. It didn't look like you."

"What was it?"

He said patiently, "It was a moonstone business . . . a necklace . . . very pretty but it lacked something. Now will you shut up and let me go to sleep?"

19

The night of the accident, Barry was at Hageney's. Hageney and his wife lived in a cluttered flat over the antique shop. Above them was another apartment, rented to a family with three children. It was always noisy at Hageney's and usually exciting. Abby was doing Nurse's Aide. She was generally home by ten.

At nine Barry left and walked home through the March night, which felt more like May, cool after the day's heat, and very like spring. The telephone was ringing furiously when he entered. He answered it, and heard a voice, almost unrecognizable. "Barry? . . . This is Craig Emerson . . . There's been an accident. . . ."

"To whom?" asked Barry. "What happened?"

"Val was driving," said Craig. "She isn't hurt, just shaken up . . . Jay Morris has a broken leg . . . Uncle Norman's pretty badly hurt, I think. Abby had better come. We're waiting for the doctor, now."

Barry said, "I'll get the first train . . . I haven't a car, and Madge is away. Abby's at the hospital. No need for her to come unless it's serious . . . I'll leave a note for her . . . And then call her, from your place."

He hung up, went to the desk, scribbled a note, standing. He ended, "Don't worry . . . Craig's an old woman; it's probably just a bruise or sprain. I'll phone you . . . sit tight until I do. . . ."

He went out and was lucky. A cruising taxi passed, stopped, and took him to the station. He had three minutes to catch the train. He caught it, and it was an express. At the Fairton station he got a cab and drove to the Wallace place. There were no cars in the driveway, but the house blazed with light; the front door was open and he walked in.

Mrs. Renning came out of the dining room. She looked harried. She said, in a whisper, "I'm so glad you came, Mr. Lambert. They've taken Mr. Morris to the hospital . . . Mr. Wallace refused to be moved."

Craig appeared on the stairs. He looked, Barry perceived, pale and anxious but brisk. He came downstairs quickly. He said, "I'm glad you didn't bring Abby, after all. It's all right. Uncle Norman wouldn't go to the hospital with Jay — There's nothing very wrong, he's shaken of course, has some bruises, and a cut or two. He threw everyone except me out of the room. A nurse is coming presently, I'll stay with him till she gets here."

"Val?"

"Oh, she's all right," said Craig carelessly. Evidently Val too had been thrown out of her husband's room, and Craig was pleased. "She always did drive like a bat out of hell," he said conversationally. "They'd gone to the library board meeting, at the Upham's, that's between here and Bluehill. Coming back she took a corner and hit a parked truck. It's a miracle that no one was killed. Sorry I didn't wait till tomorrow to call you . . . if you want to get back on the next train you can make it, I'll send you down."

Barry said, "Thanks, I'll take a look, if you don't mind, and then call Abby. I left a note, and promised I would."

"Just as you wish," said Craig. He added, "I'll go back up now. He's had a sedative, but you can look in on him. The doctor has left, he went with the ambulance. He'll be back, though."

The room was dark except for the bedside light. Norman Wallace lay in the great bed. His color looked all right to Barry, he breathed evenly as if he slept. A head bandage made him look slightly rakish.

He opened his eyes. He said, "Well, Barry!"

Barry stood beside the bed, looking down. He said, "Sorry, sir . . . but glad you're no worse off."

"I'm tough," said Wallace. "Have you seen Valentine?"

"Not yet."

"Do. She's upset. I wanted her mother to come up and stay with her, but she wouldn't have it. Is Abby here?"

Barry said, "She was at the hospital . . . I didn't want to alarm her, too much. I left a note. I'll phone her directly."

"Tell her that I'm all right." He closed his eyes, dismissing his son-in-law. Craig said softly, "Val's in her room, I believe."

Barry left the room, closing the door carefully. Val's door was shut. He knocked and she said quickly, "Who is it?"

"Barry."

She opened the door and stood looking at him. She was white under her year-round tan. She wore, attractively, not much of anything. There was a bruise on her cheek and one wrist was strapped. She asked, "Where's Abby?"

"At home," he explained. "Mind if I phone?"

This was a big room, too, and very lovely. Val had refurnished it, and it became her. Near the chaise longue where she had been lying, the telephone stood on a small table. Barry picked it up and gave his number. Waiting, he looked at Val. She had gone back to the chaise longue. There was a highball glass half empty on the table, an ash tray full of half-smoked cigarettes. On the hearth, a small fire whispered comfortingly against the little chill of the night. There were flowers in the room, photographs, the odor of perfume. . . .

Val said, "Craig thinks I did it on purpose. As if I'd be such a fool."

"Hardly," said Barry, "as you might have killed yourself. By the way, our friend Emerson didn't seem very happy to see me. Yet he sent for me."

She said, "He didn't want to; Norman insisted."

"Oh?" He raised an eyebrow and then Abby's voice jumped, literally, into his ear, small, distinct, frightened. "Barry. I've been home since ten . . . waiting — what happened?"

He said, "Your father's all right, dear, just shaken and bruised a little. No, there's a nurse on the way. I'll be home as soon as possible. There's no reason for you to come tonight, wait till tomorrow. Meantime, I'll stay till the doctor returns and talk to him."

"Jay?" she asked. "Val?"

"Jay's got a bruised leg, they tell me," Barry

said. "He's in the hospital. Sure, you can go see him. Keep your hair on, darling. I'll be home as soon as I've seen the doctor and can get a train."

He hung up and sat down on the end of the chaise longue.

"What happened," he asked, "exactly?"

Val said, "It was dark, the truck had no lights. But I wasn't going fast. Not then. If I had been, we would have been killed."

"Dim prospect," he said. "All your hard work for nothing."

Her eyes blazed. "That's a charming thing to say," she said angrily. Then she began to cry, her hands over her face. She said, "Craig — how I loathe that creeping little — he thinks, it was on purpose, he'll imply it to Norman . . . and Abby too."

"Stop yapping," said Barry. "Here, take a slug of this. He just doesn't like you, Val . . . but my father-in-law is an intelligent character. He will know that fortunate girls don't risk their beautiful necks running into trucks deliberately."

"Craig Emerson would do anything to get me out of this house," she said. She took her hands from her face and looked at him. The tears dried in the heat of anger. She added, "And I wish I *was* out of it."

"Oh, sure," said Barry, "but you'll stay . . . until Wallace goes, feet first."

Val said grimly, "I'll stay."

She set down the glass he had put in her hand. She said, "You might as well have a drink, too."

"Keep it here?" he asked, mildly amused.

"Well, no," she said, annoyed, "but there's a tray somewhere . . . and glasses."

Barry found the tray, the bottles, the ice and a glass. He poured himself a small straight shot. He asked, standing with it in his hand, "Why doesn't Craig like you?"

She said, "I don't like him. And it's simple enough. He dotes on his sinecure job here . . . if you can call it a job. It didn't suit him to have his dear Uncle Norman remarry . . . you'd married Abby, so that possibility was out for him."

"I suppose so." He added thoughtfully, "Haven't been making passes at him, have you?"

"At that jerk? Are you out of your mind?"

"No. He's not unattractive," said Barry. "Madge always said he was on the bloodless side, but I wouldn't be too sure. He's young . . . and so are you — and you are cooped up here together in this elegant foxhole, day after day."

Val said, "Do you think he'd jeopardize his position with Norman?"

"Oh," said Barry, "I catch. Out of boredom, whether you liked him or not, you did try, just for fun, just to keep your hand in? Well, that's very entertaining."

She said, "Oh, shut up, Barry, you make me tired."

He said, "It might not jeopardize his position if he didn't wave banners or send an item to the local papers. Personally, I think that Wallace encourages you to amuse yourself. How about what's his name? Your short, dark and mysterious refugee . . . the one we met last autumn? My spies saw you having a cocktail or two with him in the King Cole Room."

"Don't be silly," she said shortly.

"I'm just wondering," he told her. He put his glass down. "When do you expect the doctor?"

"After he's seen to Jay. Barry, come here. Sit down."

He sat down, found himself too close, and tried to move away but she put her hand out and took his and held it. She said, "Barry, believe me, I thought it would work."

He smiled, feeling uneasy but interested, which were very normal reactions, even for a married man in love with his wife. "This?" he inquired. "Don't you over estimate yourself or underestimate me?"

"I don't mean that. I mean . . . this house . . . Norman . . . everything. All I wanted. . . ."

"You don't want it any more?"

"No."

He said, "There's a way out, you know. Nevada, Idaho, Florida . . . several ways."

She looked at him, her dark eyes level. She said, "As long as I have it I'll hang on. I've told you that. You can fight to keep something even though you no longer want it."

"Seems senseless," he told her. "Maybe I'll hate myself for asking, but what do you want, Mrs. W.?"

She said, "You. I've always wanted you, Barry."

She pulled him toward her, so suddenly that he almost lost his balance. He thought, wildly, First time in my life I've been more kissed than kissing. He couldn't deny that it was an experience. Yet not too convincing. Why? He thought, holding her closer, a purely reflex gesture, he assured himself, Why? Or, why not?

Someone turned the door knob and Val removed herself from Barry's vicinity. Craig looked in. He regarded the room, and he looked at Val, the glasses, and at Barry. He said, "The doctor just drove up . . . thought you'd like to know."

The door closed, definitely. Barry said, "Well."

Val spoke. She said, "He'll run to Norman, I suppose."

"What is there to tell?" asked Barry. "You needed – consolation. I was being solicitous."

She asked, "Hadn't you better go talk to the doctor?"

On the following day Abby came up to Fairton. Barry had brought her a satisfactory report from the doctor and suggested that she wait a few days before seeing her father. But she had said, "I wouldn't feel comfortable about it, Barry." And he had argued no more, watching her across the breakfast table, thinking how lovely she was, how vulnerable and young. He said casually:

"Val was in a spin. She believes that Emerson thinks she wrecked the car, incidentally breaking Jay's leg . . . deliberately . . . fancying herself as an eligible young widow."

"That," said Abby, "is pretty silly, as she might have killed herself too."

"Which I too pointed out." He looked at his orange juice. Nice color, orange juice. He started to say, And when I was trying to calm her, Craig crashed in. He's convinced he saw a powerful love scene in the making.

Well, say it, once over lightly. But he couldn't. The words stuck in his throat.

He washed them down with the orange juice. He thought, Yet if Craig gets to her first? He cleared his throat. He said:

"I waited in Val's room, after seeing your father . . . until the doctor returned. She was pretty shaken up . . . she'd had a drink or two, into the bargain."

For once, Abby wasn't thinking of Val. She was thinking of Jay Morris, poor little man, his bones old and brittle . . . so she said indifferently, "Val was being dramatic, I suppose. She can't stand Craig . . . she's told me a dozen times. It sounds ridiculous, but I believe they're jealous of each other."

After that, you couldn't say more. What was there to say? "Val took a turn for the amorous, and in popped our boy friend, and no doubt I looked guilty as hell."

He said nothing further.

20

Norman Wallace's nurse was middle-aged and efficient. She was not impressed by her patient, his house, or his fabulous collection. She was, however, somewhat, and unfavorably, impressed by his young wife who, after Mrs. Heddon's arrival on the previous evening, had rapped not once but several times upon the patient's door and suggested admittance. Mrs. Heddon had quite naturally admitted her, although reminding her gently that Mr. Wallace was sleeping. He woke, however, between the second and third visits and spoke with surprising strength. He said, "I'd rather not have anyone in here again tonight, Mrs. Heddon."

Mrs. Heddon, who had formed what she thought of as An Opinion of young women in transparent peach-colored negligees and elderly husbands who obviously didn't know how to pick wives, or automobile drivers, was, therefore, pleased to tell Mrs. Wallace upon her third appearance that the patient could not be disturbed.

Val was downstairs when Abby drove up from the station. She came into the hall to meet her, the bruise darkening on her cheek, her sprained wrist strapped. Otherwise, she looked much as usual, but there were creases between her brows. She took Abby's arm and said, "Before you go upstairs — wait till you see the dragon in charge! — come in here a moment."

They went into the small reception room, and Val sat down. She said, "What I've been through!"

Abby asked, "How is Father?"

"All right. Mrs. Heddon — that's the nurse — permitted me to see him for a moment this morning. She'll probably give you five minutes, looking meaningly at her watch all the time. He ate a good breakfast, she says."

"Have you heard from Jay?"

"I telephoned. He's as comfortable as possible . . . Abby, you don't blame me, do you?"

Abby said coolly, "For what?"

"The accident. I didn't see the damned truck. And I wasn't going fast, as events proved. That idiot Craig practically accused me of driving sixty, seventy an hour — as if I'd wanted to crack up the car."

Abby said, "I know. Barry told me. It

couldn't be more absurd."

"Well," said Val, "I'm glad you feel that way. Craig Emerson has a nasty little mind. He hates me and he'd do anything to estrange me from Norman."

Abby asked, "How could he? I think you're hysterical, Val. May I see Father now?"

Val said, "If it hadn't been for Barry's coming last night I would have been out of my mind."

Abby remembered Barry talking to her about Val at breakfast, saying, Val was in a spin; Val had had a couple of drinks. She said mechanically, "Naturally, you were upset," and moved toward the door. Val did not follow her, she sat there, pulling a handkerchief between her fingers, watching Abby walk into the hall.

It wasn't going well, she thought, not well at all. The accident had been just that. Yet it could have been turned to advantage . . . only, it hadn't been. And what, she wondered, was wrong with Norman? She knew him well enough to know that had he wanted to see her, a dozen Mrs. Heddons couldn't have stopped him while he remained in possession of his faculties.

Mrs. Heddon did not remain in the room with Abby. She had her orders. She looked with astonishment at her when she came in, and Wallace made the presentations. Here was someone really impressive. She thought, I've never seen such hair. She was not a Fairton woman, she came from the hospital a number of miles distant. She had never seen the Wallaces before. When her patient had said, "My daughter is coming from New York this morning, Mrs. Heddon," she had pictured a woman of her own age or, at the most, in her thirties.

Abby smiled at her. "You must tell me when my time's up," she said.

Mrs. Heddon thought, Well, bless you, you're not much more than twenty and the prettiest thing I ever saw. Aloud she said, "Shall we say half an hour, Mrs. Lambert? Your father's doing fine. But he mustn't get overtired."

The door closed and Wallace said, "You look a little puzzled."

"It's nothing," she said. "I'm so glad you weren't badly hurt." She was. She had suffered authentically between reading Barry's note and hearing his voice on the telephone. She could not rationalize it. It was plain biology, probably. She had once loved her father, she had been hurt by him, she had feared him, and even bitterly disliked him. She had, more recently schooled herself to indifference, but when she had learned that he had been injured her blood spoke to her in a voice she could not ignore, the voice of compassion.

"I'm tough," he said, as he had said to Barry. "Valentine was quite remarkable, really. She kept her head. It was not her fault."

"She's afraid you might think it so."

His gray lips twitched into a smile. "That's Craig," he said, "a good boy but oversolicitous . . . or" – his voice trailed off; he added mildly – "you say things you don't mean when you are frightened."

"Val frightened me a little," said Abby. "I thought you were – worse. She said she wasn't allowed in for long this morning."

Her father moved his head on the pillows. He said, "My orders – confidentially. Valentine is a little overpowering, when one isn't quite up to scratch. She was badly shaken herself but she has an exuberance, a vitality that can triumph over that, or anything. You, Abby, are extremely restful. Did anyone ever tell you that?"

"No," she said; "and I don't believe it, really."

He said carefully, "It was kind of Barry to come last night, sensible of him to keep you away until he knew exactly how things were. Also, he was a comfort to Valentine. You see, she doesn't like Craig."

Abby said uncomfortably, "Well, they aren't exactly each other's type."

"As good a way to put it as any." He closed his eyes. He looked very old and tired. He said,

267

after a moment, "I have been thinking that perhaps it would be a good thing if Craig took a little holiday. He works hard, and faithfully. But he and Valentine get on each other's nerves, rather, and create a feeling of tension that disturbs me."

Oh, no, thought Abby, you mustn't; that's just what she wants you to do! She felt a sharp irritation with Craig, who could permit himself to be maneuvered into this position. But her father went on, without opening his eyes:

"You don't approve of that? But in this instance I am thinking of myself." He opened his eyes and they were very cold and quiet. "I can hardly send my wife away," he reminded her. "It's quite possible that once Craig has had time to relax away from Fairton, he will see the situation in the right light. There are always compromises. Life's built on them!"

Abby asked cautiously, "But what situation could there be?"

"Abby," said her father, "you are not a child, you are a married woman. Do not be willfully — shall we say, innocent? Valentine is an attractive young woman. She has more sex appeal — which is a cliché but suffices — than almost any other woman I have ever known. Craig does not like her, and he was greatly distressed when we married. However, she attracts him. It is wholly natural if not estimable. He fights, as the attraction is abhorrent to him; also, it frightens him. So he goes on disliking her, all the more as he becomes more involved — emotionally." He hesitated, asked, "Is that the right word? I don't think so. Physically is better."

"For heaven's sake, Father," Abby began, "who has been —"

"No one has to tell me things of this sort," interrupted Wallace. "I sit on the side lines and observe. I've been doing it a lifetime. I am not distressed by this, my dear. Valentine is capable of handling it and, moreover, *she* is not involved. She doesn't like poor Craig, and the reason is simple. She had no interest in him as a man and resents his quasi-filial position in the household. It's all quite logical. But I feel it would do no harm, and probably good, if Craig were to take a little trip. So I've arranged it. He's going to Sea Island for some golf and, I hope, an enjoyable visit. I told him this morning."

"Does — does he want to go?"

"On the contrary." He closed his eyes again. "But I have persuaded him. It will please Valentine. And by the time he returns the accident will have been forgotten except, of course, by Jay. However, the doctor assured me that he has the very best of care, that the break was a clean one, and in the course of time he will be very nearly as good as new. Are you planning to see him?"

She said, "This afternoon."

"Good enough," said her father. "Craig will drive you over. He will then have someone to whom he can complain." He smiled again. Then he said, "I haven't been wholly truthful with you, Abby."

She looked at him, startled.

"About what?"

He said, "It has little or nothing to do with the accident. My heart was not particularly good before that. Last night did not help it perhaps, but it did it no lasting harm."

"Your *heart*," she said, "but I never — "

He said, "I shall be honest now. I have had for some time a cardiac condition. It is the sort of thing you can live with for a very long time if you take care of yourself. I have always done that, as you know; I am temperate, take no undue exercises. Last night's affair has set me back somewhat, but I shall recover. I have said nothing to Craig or Val, and of course, Barry. The doctor is a sensible man. He made his report, at my request, solely on the basis of the accident."

She asked, "Why are you telling me — now?"

"I am trying to make you understand something . . . my marriage, principally." He looked very tired now but went on doggedly. "We won't go into the things you must have thought, and still think. You were gone, I was lonelier than I cared to admit. Valentine is very entertaining. I enjoy looking at her, and observing the processes of her mind, even those she believes she hides from me. Ours was not a conventional marriage by any standard, a man in his middle seventies, a girl in her twenties. It has, I dare say, its revolting aspects . . . to you and," he added thoughtfully, "particularly to Barry." He raised his hand. "Don't interrupt me," he said, "please. Yes, particularly to Barry. You would not understand that as you are not, my dear, a young and virile male. However, that is not the point of this dissertation. I married Valentine in order to be less lonely and to amuse myself. I am quite fond of her. I was aware that when we made our bargain I did her almost as much of an injustice as if the marriage had been conventional. But she understood the bargain; and also that in the nature of things, and the face of statistics, she was likely to be a widow longer than she had been − as the phrase goes − a wife." He paused, to rest.

Abby said, "Bargain?"

He said, "Naturally. Did you think for a moment that I was interested in an intimate relationship? A relationship which never has been a factor, with me. Not even when I was a quarter of a century younger. Certainly, not now. I could not ask Valentine to live in my house unless I married her, conventions being what they are."

She said quickly, "Father, I'd rather you didn't —"

"Of course, you'd rather. But I wish you to know. Also, Valentine married me for whatever I could give her, she has been, so far, content enough. She knows exactly how far she can go in her search for diversion if she is bored . . . as she often must be — and where — for the time being, that is, for as long as I live — she must stop. You aren't liking this, are you?"

"I'm hating it," said Abby, stifled. "It's . . ."

"Cold-blooded? Quite. Yet I would have thought you'd prefer it to a feeble whipping up of ancient blood to temporary heat," he said, amused.

Abby said, "If you wouldn't . . . you're tired, please don't talk any more."

He said, "Very well. But so far Val hasn't repented of her bargain, I think." He struggled to sit up and Abby rose and helped him, her arm about him, the pillows rearranged under her deft hands.

"Thank you," he said. He added, "Will you believe that I married Valentine mainly to protect you, Abby?"

Mrs. Heddon knocked before she could answer, and came in. Wallace looked at her amiably. He said, "Mrs. Lambert was just leaving, Mrs. Heddon. I'll see her, after she has been to the hospital to call on Mr. Morris. Abby, just a minute, would you and Barry consider coming up for a time? If Barry cannot take a week or two off from his work, perhaps he would be willing to commute. Helpful as Valentine has been, she cannot take your place and Craig's too. I'm a little pressed for time, with the book, now that Anderson is to publish it, and you could be very useful. You could," he added, anticipating her excuses, "put in your hospital hours here . . . Morton or Valentine would drive you over. Think about it. It would please me — very much."

Luncheon was an uneasy occasion with Craig glowering, Val pushing her plate away, crying, "I simply can't eat. That Heddon woman is impossible. If Norman isn't in danger, why must he be guarded as if he were on the critical list?" She left, abruptly, before the meal was over. She said, "I'm sorry . . . but I feel utterly foul. Give Jay my love, Abby, and tell him I'll come see him as soon as possible. Poor little man, he must hate me."

After she had left, Craig looked at Abby. He

273

repeated, "Poor little man," in Val's exact accents. Abby shook her head at him in warning. They weren't alone, the luncheon service continued, and once Mrs. Renning popped in, anxious and abstracted, to see if everything was all right.

Craig drove Abby to the hospital. He said nothing as the station wagon creaked down the drive, but once on the public road he flared out at her. "Did your father tell you," he demanded, "that he's sending me away?"

"Only for a rest," she reminded him soothingly.

"I don't need a rest. Yes, I do; who doesn't? But I don't *want* one. It's Val, of course. She's persuaded him."

"When did he tell you he wanted you to go?" Abby asked.

"This morning. I saw him just long enough for that. I couldn't argue. He simply closed his eyes at me and Mrs. Heddon shooed me out."

She said, "Val's hardly seen him either, so I doubt if she made any attempt to —"

He asked angrily, "Are you on her side? Abby, you're an idiot."

"Thanks, too much."

"I didn't mean . . . I'm on edge. Sorry. But naturally, it's her strategy. Not since the accident; before. Anything to get me out of the house. I tell you, she has an ungodly influence over him. Last week he had a junior partner in his law firm up here." He shot a glance at her. "Malcolm. Remember?"

"Perfectly," she said with tranquillity. "How is he . . . how does he look?"

"Fine, fat and prosperous," Craig answered, "as a man usually looks when he marries the boss's daughter. Abby, Val's trying to make Uncle Norman change his will . . . I'm certain of it."

"Oh, Craig," said Abby wearily.

Craig said, "Well, why should I be nasty-nice about it? He always promised me that when he died I'd have enough to establish my own gallery . . . he trained me for it. Jay was to have an annuity. It's incredible," he added, "that you have no interest in what happens to the money."

She said, "I don't care . . . neither does Barry."

"No one," said Craig, "ever had too much. If you hadn't been so besotted —"

"I don't like that word."

"Well, preoccupied, then, with your own affairs, you would have done something about this — this obscene marriage."

Abby laughed suddenly. She had taken off her hat and the March sun was warm and golden on her hair. She asked, "What, for instance? I didn't consult Father when I married. It wasn't likely he'd consult me."

He said angrily, "Why didn't you come up last night?"

"Barry said it wasn't necessary."

"It wasn't," said Craig, "yet it would have been a natural gesture. Why didn't he bring you with him?"

"I've answered that."

"Oh, sure, and now you're sore at me. But Barry came up fast enough," said Craig, "to console his ex-girl friend."

Abby sat very still. After a moment she said, "That was a stupid remark."

"I saw them," said Craig, "I went to Val's room to tell her and Barry that Dr. Lansing had returned. They were having a very cozy time . . . drinks on the house, and —"

She said sharply, "That's enough, I think."

"Okay."

They were silent the rest of the way. Abby sat with her hands in her lap. She saw forsythia spilling like sunshine over the gray stone walls, she saw the wild fruit trees in snowy, early bloom; the wind was soft against her flushed cheeks and the sky a flawless blue.

She thought, Craig's just — being vicious. And her father had given her at least one reason why. Val. Craig himself had provided another:

the altered will, if the will had been altered. She closed her mind against Craig as she would have closed a door between herself and a stormy night.

When they reached the hospital, high on the hill above a busy small town, "I'm sorry," he said.

"That's all right. You coming in with me?"

"Of course."

The corridors smelled as most hospital corridors smell; the nurses were overworked, as are most nurses. Fortunately, there had been a room for Jay . . . small, but sunny. He lay in bed, looking much as ever, dry and sardonic, but his leg monstrous in its splints and what he called "rigging."

Abby bent to kiss his forehead. She said, "This is a fine business."

They sat down and he smiled at them. He asked, "How's Norman?"

Abby told him. He nodded. He said, "Glad he's all right. I wasn't quite sure . . . Dr. Lansing might have been soft-pedaling."

"Are you in much pain?" asked Abby.

"Enough. But they have ways of helping. Tell Norman I won't need special nurses after today."

"You'll have them as long as the hospital will let us keep them on," said Abby. "I like the day one . . . she's cute."

"Wasted on me," said Jay, "the cuteness, I mean."

She said, "Val sent her love. She'll come see you when she can."

"Probably ashamed to," said Craig briefly.

Jay Morris shook his head. He said, "It wasn't her fault. I hear they are holding the truck driver for negligence or something."

Craig said doggedly, "Val drives too fast."

"Wasn't at the time," said Jay. "Abby, don't look so worried. I'm all right. Where's your husband?"

"He came up last night," said Abby, "but wouldn't let me come till today. He's in New York, now."

Jay said, "With me laid up, Craig, you'll have your work cut out for you."

"Not me," said Craig. "Uncle Norman is shipping me off to Sea Island for, quote, a well-earned holiday, unquote."

Jay looked from Craig to Abby. He said, after a moment, "That's fine . . . but, without us both —? I'll be laid up for quite a while — what does your father expect to do, Abby?"

"He's asked me to come up for a few weeks," Abby answered.

Craig stared at her. "You didn't tell me . . ." he began.

Abby said, "You gave me little opportunity." She looked at Jay. "What do you think?"

The old man scowled. He said, "Sounds like a good idea. As long as they keep me here, Abby, I'll stew. You can be liaison officer between me and Norman."

She suggested hesitantly, "There's Val."

Both men were silent. Then Jay said casually, "Mrs. Wallace hasn't done much work on the book lately. There's been a good deal of entertaining. Craig took over, for the most part."

"What she knows about it, except for taking shorthand," said Craig, "you could put in your eye and feel no pain. That was — façade, Abby, and you know it."

She said uneasily, "She's interested a publisher."

Craig shrugged. "She could do that," he agreed, "if he's a man."

Jay did not like intimate conversations. He was a man without intimates. He liked being that way. Paintings were more satisfactory than people. They did not alter; they never talked back; they didn't argue, gossip or speculate; and there were hard and fast rules, by which anyone who had the necessary patience to become an expert could ascertain authenticity and evaluate them. With people you were never sure.

He said, "I wish you were an aide here, Abby, it would be very pleasant for me."

Abby and Craig left a little later. On the way back, he asked her, "Are you coming up to stay?"

"I'll have to talk to Barry."

He said, "I don't know how to advise you."

"I haven't," she reminded him, "asked for your advice."

"Naturally. Yet I'll give it. On the one hand, it would be sensible for you to keep an eye on things," he told her flatly. "Matters would be better between you and Uncle Norman; he wouldn't be so easily influenced from outside. On the other hand. . . ."

"Well?"

"On both hands, it comes down to Val," he said.

Abby waited.

He said, "You aren't of much help . . . I don't know why I bother to say this. It might be better if I kept my mouth shut. Certainly, opening it isn't to my advantage. But I care more about you than anyone else in the world. That's the way it is, take it or leave it. I don't like Barry. Why should I? For almost a year I've liked him less and less. Yet putting all that aside and thinking only of you, I don't think you'd be very smart if you exposed him to

Val . . . day in, day out."

Craig had been exposed to her, day in, day out.

Abby said, "That's not only silly, Craig, it's malicious."

He said again, "Take it or leave it."

When they reached Fairton, Craig waited while she went upstairs to say good-bye to her father. Val's door was shut. Abby did not knock on it. She knocked on Wallace's door instead and Mrs. Heddon admitted her. She said, "He's had a good nap and some nourishment . . ." and slipped away, smiling.

Standing by the bed Abby made her report on Jay. He wasn't in too much pain. She had talked to the nurse. It would take time, his were not young bones; but he'd be all right. Wallace listened, and said, "He's to have every comfort, I told Dr. Lansing that; I'm telling you so that you'll see to it." He added, "You will come up, won't you, Abby?"

She said, as she had to Craig, "I'll have to talk to Barry," But she added, "Val mightn't like it, father."

"Valentine?" His eyes were amused, "Why not?"

"It's a fairly delicate situation, isn't it? After all, this is her house. She gives the orders."

"It's mine," he said calmly, "and I give them.

You won't be encroaching upon her privileges, my dear. You'll help me. Craig will be away, and Jay. That means I'll need someone to take over in the gallery."

"The gallery?" she asked. She had forgotten the public Thursdays.

He reminded her. "Craig won't be here to look after visitors," he said.

"I hadn't thought of that. Why don't you withdraw the offer . . . now that you are ill? People will understand. Besides, I thought, not many come."

"They did at first, mainly out of curiosity. But some, with a real interest, still come. And they — however few — must be conducted through the gallery by someone who knows the paintings. Val is intelligent and has picked up a considerable smattering, but even if she wished she could hardly act as guide."

Before she could answer he said, "Talk it over with Barry, then. I hope he will be amenable."

21

Abby reached home late in the afternoon, and the telephone rang shortly after she had washed the dust from her face and hands. It was Barry. How was her father, and Jay? Good. Val too? "That's fine," he said. He added that he'd be late. She must be tired . . . why not meet him at the Italian joint – whatever she had planned for dinner would keep, wouldn't it?

She reached the restaurant first and waited at their corner table. It was a good little place. It no longer served lavish slices of spiced sausage, the elegant veal dishes were rarely on the menu . . . and the steaks and chops, which had served as a concession to American tastes, were no longer to be found. Chicken was a rarity, but the spaghetti was as delicious and filling as ever, and the meat sauce was still meat. The green salads were very special, raviolis abounded, and the wine was good.

Barry came tearing in, and sat down. He said, "Hi," and looked at her. That kind of look was almost as satisfactory as a kiss. He commented, "You look bushed. Better have a drink. I'll order."

The waiter came, smiling; the order was given.

Barry leaned back. He said, "Give."

She reported, first on the medical side. "Poor old Jay," she said, her eyes clouding. "He's had, and will have, a wretched time."

"You couldn't kill him with a bazooka, honey," said Barry. The drinks had come, and he lifted his glass. "To us," he said.

Abby tasted her cocktail, set it down. She said, "Father wants us to come out and live with him for a while."

"My God, why? As protection against Val?" asked Barry, amused.

She explained: Craig's holiday — at which Barry quirked an eyebrow; the notes for the book; the gallery.

"Do you want it that way?" asked Barry.

She looked at him, an open regard. "Not very much," she admitted.

"Well then, hell, say no. You have an excuse . . . I could come only weekends. But I have to go through the motions of my job, and besides, the law class."

She said, "I don't see how I could stand it without you."

"You don't have to. I don't get it, anyway," he said. "Sounds okay on the surface, I suppose. But —"

She said, tentatively, "Craig advised me to say no, too. He said you shouldn't be exposed to Val!"

"He said that? Handsome of him," said Barry. "What a character."

"He seems to think she's . . . an unexploded bomb," said Abby.

"I've seen 'em," said Barry briefly, "and avoided 'em."

She hesitated; then made up her mind, told him what her father had said of Val and Craig. Barry looked less astonished than she had expected. He remarked, after a moment, "Well, it's logical enough. Explains Emerson's solicitude for me, perhaps. Bomb exploded in *his* face."

"If I don't go," said Abby, "Craig will think —"

"What do you care what he thinks?"

"I don't." She lifted her chin. All day she had thought of one phrase of her father's; one he had not bothered to explain . . . "I married Valentine to protect you," he had said. From whom, from what?

"Then," asked Barry, as their order came, "what's the matter with you? Write your father, say you can't leave town . . . and me." He grinned. "I'll beat you if you do. Tell him that."

She said slowly, "You're out a good deal. I'd see almost as much of you if I do go. . . ."

He put down his fork. "What's this leading up to?" he demanded, "and besides, it isn't true . . . How about breakfast, and long before breakfast?"

She said, "Craig doesn't want me to go."

"So you've said."

"I don't know about Val . . . it wasn't discussed with her."

He said, "Oh, for Pete's sake, Val wouldn't care."

"You know her better than I do," said Abby.

"What does that mean? Make up your mind; if you want to go, go ahead. You're grown up, I hope; you can make up your mind. And it's nothing to me what you do about it. Okay, one way or the other."

"Nothing to you? You mean you wouldn't mind?"

"Don't twist things," he said irritably. "God, how like a woman. Sure, I'd mind. I'd miss you like the devil. But if you want to go, do so . . . but don't make an issue of it . . . dragging in Emerson, Val, all the rest. If you want to come all over filial, that's all right by me. I don't see how the old so-and-so rates it but . . . hey, were you thinking about the will?"

She had told him that too. She hadn't been thinking about it.

"No, and I don't believe it," she said. "Craig probably just dreamed it up because Malcolm came out."

"Malcolm . . . Oh, that guy." He looked at her and grinned. "Thinking you might run into him again?" he teased genially, "raking up an ember or two? I'll break his damned neck."

She laughed, warmed, somewhat happier. "Thanks. I wasn't thinking about him, though."

He said, "If there's anything in this will business, maybe you'd better stick around awhile."

"But you've never cared about the money," she reminded him.

"No, that's a fact. But I haven't any right to prevent you from looking after your interests, darling. It would have been no hair off my hide if your father had cut you off with a dime when we married . . . I could look after you. But if he didn't then, and if he is planning some shenanigans now — needled by Val — you'd be a dope to sit back and say, Let her have the lot. Anything could happen to me. I might get bumped off by a taxi, or an opponent. Madge might erase Bob via Reno and remarry . . . someone who'd be sure to outlive her; the Elson estate could go to pot. Get me straight, I wouldn't raise a hand, literally, to rescue an antique dollar of the Wallace dough, as far as its usefulness to me is concerned. But it would be damned unjust to you, at this juncture, if your father grew whimsical."

"You're advising me to go?"

"Nope."

She considered a moment. She said presently, "I think I'll go then, Barry."

"Okay," he said. "it's your headache. You aren't eating. Thought you were hungry."

"I thought so too," she said, "I felt caved in. But I don't now."

She lay long awake that night . . . listening to Barry's even breathing. She thought, I believed I knew him . . . or was beginning to know him . . . that he was no longer a stranger. Yet, every now and then. . . .

Why hadn't he been angry, or, if not angry, amused when she told him what Craig said, about Val . . . about keeping Barry away from Val? He hadn't been either . . . just, not quite.

She hadn't told him the other thing Craig had said . . . "Barry came up fast enough to console his ex-girl friend."

Her small jaw tightened. She thought, Craig knows I'm afraid of her . . . she changed the word quickly ... that I distrust her. He's jealous ... of her position in the house; he hates her because, if what Father said is true, she attracts him. He's jealous of Barry.

She thought drearily of the house in Fairton, and the people who would come to it; of meals with Val and her father; of hours in the library; of the wild, young spring green on the hills and in the gardens ... of seeing Barry weekends and never alone until they were shut away from the others in their room. She couldn't go. She told herself, Tomorrow I'll tell Barry I've changed my mind.

Val telephoned, while Abby was getting breakfast.

"Watch the toast," she told Barry, running to the phone, "and don't let the coffee perk more than two minutes longer. Hello ..." Her voice changed. "Val — has anything happened?"

Val said, "Everything's fine. Norman told me just now that he'd asked you to come up ... I wish you would, it would be wonderful. But I know how you feel about leaving Barry. Norman would kill me if he knew I was crossing him, he's so anxious to have you ... especially as, after he's up and about, I have to be in and out of town, quite a bit — clothes," she said vaguely, "decorations and such. But I can manage, darling, and even bone up on the collection to impress the visiting firemen."

Abby said, "Thanks a lot, Val, but I've decided to come . . . next week. I'll finish out the week here, and make some arrangements to go on with my hospital work up there as Father suggested. I talked it over with Barry and he wants me to do as I wish."

"Well," said Val, "that's swell . . . for me, I mean . . . I just didn't want you to sacrifice yourself. I'll tell Norman. He'll be delighted."

"What's on her mind, if anything?" asked Barry, coming in with the percolator. "Think I overdid it a minute or so," he said apologetically.

Abby turned from the telephone table. She said, "Val was calling to tell me I needn't come . . . as far as she was concerned. She can manage . . . she put me in my place. Very nicely, of course."

"Which double makes up your mind for you, natch," said Barry, grinning.

"That's right," said Abby. "The coffee looks as if you could walk on it."

"Want me to try?" He added, "Women are wonderful."

Abby smiled faintly, her face closed against him. He thought uneasily, I don't like this. I wish she wouldn't go . . . I've half a mind. . . .

But only half. He began tentatively, "Look, kid, if Val gets under your skin, why not call it off?"

She asked gently, "Not scared, are you?"

He jumped up, pulled her out of the chair, and shook her hard. Her hair slipped from the few, treasured pins and fell about her shoulders. He kissed her. He said, "Must you be a so-and-so?"

"Feline? Feminine? Barry, my pins," she wailed. "They're harder to get than Scotch!"

He helped her retrieve them. He commented, as he straightened up, "When I said I would miss you it was a masterpiece of understatement."

22

April was rain and wind and frost; April was March as it should have been, cold and cloudy and biting at your bones. Mrs. Renning sighed every time she turned up the thermostat. Craig had departed. Jay Morris was still in the hospital. Val went to town, came back again. . . .

Abby worked with her father in the library or took people through the gallery on Thursdays. She saw Jay every day, either as a visitor or as a nurse's aide. Barry came up Fridays, and left early Monday morning. Lying alone in her own bedroom, Abby could almost imagine she was back there for good . . . but not quite . . . not while she missed Barry as she did.

Madge wrote from Hot Springs, in italics. "What in the *world* are you *doing* there? Are you out of your *mind?* Leaving Barry alone like that. How is Val? I hope you keep her in her place, *whatever* it is . . ." She added what she thought it was, also italicized, and censorable.

"But as long as you're there," she went on, "you might as well run over to the place now and then and see if it's burned down or if those people are robbing me blind. I'm staying here, though Bob is *very* fretful. It's good for me, and I hear the weather's foul at home. It could be better here but we've found some amusing people and there's a quite divine creature, just out of the Air Force, who dances as well as he flies. Bob glowers It's *fun*."

Barry read it, groaning. He said, "Don't tell me . . . not when I've become used to Bob!"

Once Barry managed to come up, midweek, for the night. He'd run into Val, he explained, just as he was buzzing out of the station, having picked up a reservation for his boss. "The office boys," he said sadly, "are fighting the war." He'd thought, Why not, no class tonight. Would his father-in-law offer him some pajamas? How was the toothbrush situation? They'd just made the train. No time to phone, much less to get to the apartment and pick up his duffle.

Abby's delight, so unexpected, so sharp that it was almost painful, was tempered by Val's expression . . . a little smug, a little cream-on-whiskers. She was also looking lovely. A new suit, a wide-brimmed hat. She was having numerous fittings these days, in the city. She observed that she really shouldn't . . . she had plenty of clothes . . . it was practically unpatriotic, but "Norman insists," she said.

They were in the drawing room, before dinner. Wallace nursed his sherry glass, Barry took a second Martini. A fire snapped on the hearth, and it had begun to rain, rain that was half sleet.

Wallace said tolerantly, "Don't be apologetic, Valentine . . . the picture deserves its frame." He smiled and Barry said, "Speaking as a patriot, sir, and One of Our Boys, I freely admit that if decorative women were to be rationed, I would patronize the black market."

Mondays, Val usually went to town with Barry, but if she was in the city Fridays, they came up together. A natural arrangement, Abby told herself, and told herself twice, the time that Barry found he could take an earlier train and telephoned Val. "Chased her all over the damned town, dressmaker to decorator," he said. "I said, how's about it, baby? Let's scram out of here . . . I'll buy you a drink first."

Perfectly natural.

Toward the end of the month, as the peace rumors increased and nerves were tighter, when radios were turned on early and left on late, Abby went to town for the first time since she had come to her father's. He sent her to attend an auction, as his proxy. It was Friday, and she went in with Val, who was having final fittings. They had arranged to meet Barry at the station and take the five-o'clock.

They reached New York about eleven-thirty. Val asked, going up the ramp. "Let's hope we can get a taxi . . . I'll drop you – where? Or, you drop me."

"You go on," said Abby, "you've only ten minutes to make your appointment . . . and I've a phone call to make."

"Barry?" asked Val, and smiled. She patted Abby's arm. She said, "Abby – do you know . . . I wouldn't . . ." Abby watched her walk through the station, not hurrying. People turned to look. There were whistles from an appreciative group of servicemen.

She went to the telephone and called Barry at his office. She said, "It's me, darling . . . I was going to try to get my hair washed . . . which takes practically forever. But if you can get away for lunch, I'll skip it . . . Or, if you can't, could you come to the auction? We might have tea or something before traintime."

He was tied up, he said. He'd see her at the gate, ten minutes before traintime. "Have a good day," he told her.

She was able to have her hair washed, someone had broken an appointment. The man Madge had sent her to, in town, was very good.

He handled her hair with impersonal pleasure. It was wonderful hair ... how clever of her never to cut it, never to have a hot iron, a permanenting machine near it. ...

She had time only for a sandwich and milk in a crowded place before she went to the auction. She had meant to shop, a little.

Her head ached. If she knew Barry was coming, that they would be together, even in this crowd, it would be better.

Stuffy in the auction rooms. She felt a little dizzy and confused ... the sandwich perhaps ... it had had a strange taste.

The first of the paintings she had been instructed to bid upon came up for sale.

The afternoon wore on. She saw people she knew, collectors or their agents, owners of commercial galleries. With two of the paintings, a Breughel and a small Corot, she was successful. She paid a little less than her father had instructed. With the third she was less fortunate, there were higher bids.

She left, and there remained over an hour before traintime, She felt giddy still, slightly seasick. She had a sudden longing for her funny little apartment with its lack of luxury and its crazy rooftop above the noisy street. If she could get a cab she could go down for half an hour; pick up a few things she had forgotten to take with her and which, no matter how often she reminded Barry, he forgot too . . . the Toledo work combs she sometimes wore; the belt for her white dinner dress.

She found a cab, outside the auction rooms, and drove to the apartment. She met one of Hageney's best workers as she was going up the steps, a tall spare woman. They spoke and Mrs. Eaton said, "We've missed you. I've told Mr. Lambert to be sure and tell you every time I've seen him."

Pleasant to be missed; to feel that she was slowly becoming part of Barry's pattern, a pattern into which Mrs. Eaton fitted. Abby went lightly up the stairs. Someone had a radio on, in the flat below. It made a terrific noise, shouting that victory was nearer every day, victory in Europe. . . .

She put her key in the lock.

Val. Val and Barry. Sitting together on the couch . . . their glasses making rings on the table in front of them . . . Val had been crying. Her powder was streaked, her lipstick blurred. There was lipstick on Barry too, on his collar, on his cheek. . . .

Abby spoke, as Barry jumped to his feet, and Val, her devastated face shocked into surprise, raised her hands automatically to her disheveled hair.

Abby said, pitifully, "Barry — you wouldn't come to the auction room. . . ."

Something happens; something you dreaded, yet could not believe; something about which you had been warned, obliquely or openly, and what do you do?

You say the first thing that enters your bewildered mind, trivial, or absurd. You seize upon it; it is important; it has to be because what is really important doesn't bear thinking about.

Abby had a sense of disintegration . . . as if she were falling apart, her tight little world, with her, a world both heaven and earth.

No private heaven? No heaven at all, not ever.

Her face was crumpled as a weeping child's, but she did not cry. Her eyes were dry, they could see; they saw the quick relief in Barry's eyes; Val's slowly returning self-confidence.

"Abby," said Barry, and came toward her, "darling . . . I know this looks a little —"

Val interrupted. "Abby . . . I called Barry . . . I asked him to see me, where we could talk alone . . . he had to help me. . . ."

Abby walked past them. She didn't look at them. She heard what they said. It made no sense. She went into the bathroom and locked the door. Her hands were cold but there was sweat on her palms, her forehead, all over her body. The bathroom was a dark little place.

Darker now, but dizzy with flashes of light.

Her knees shook and hopelessness seized her; it was, at the moment, purely physical. She was very thoroughly sick.

Barry was hammering on the door. He was shouting . . . "Let me in, Abby, for God's sake!"

She sat on the floor and put her forehead against the cold rim of the tub. She shook, inside. But her hands were steadier. She felt better; the sickness had passed, physically. After a while she got up and took a bottle of mouthwash from the shelf. She rinsed her mouth. Then she washed her face. There was powder on the shelf, and a lipstick. She used them.

Barry had stopped hammering. Now, in the living room, he was shouting at Val. "Of all the damned, crazy . . . she's sick, I tell you. . . ."

Abby unlocked the door and walked out. Barry came through the living room and took her by the shoulders. He said, "You'll listen to me."

She looked at him; and he let her go. She said, "I'm going back to Fairton . . . you can do as you please."

She went out then . . . nothing Val could say, and she tried to say something, and nothing Barry could say or do, would stop her. The door closed.

Barry picked up his highball glass. There was still a little in it. He shattered it, on the floor. The gesture released the tension in him. He said, "That's torn it."

Val was almost herself. She said. "Don't be dramatic. She'll get over it . . . you'll explain —"

"Till I am blue in the face," he assured her. "Where will it get me . . . even if she says she believes me . . . if there's always a doubt. . . ?"

"That's her hard luck," said Val coolly.

He said, "She hasn't grown up."

"To do her justice, no woman ever grows up sufficiently to face what looks like a situation."

"It doesn't only look like it," he said gloomily.

Val said, "Well, I tried. . . ."

"Sure, you tried."

They were silent. He walked around the room. He did not look at the portrait above the mantel. The portrait was Abby; but the eyes were empty of fear or shock, empty of reproach; the face was quiet; there was radiance in it, because the painter had loved the subject.

"What do we do next?" asked Val.

He said, "We get the hell out of here and to Fairton."

"She may have missed the train," said Val. "There isn't another one until around six."

"We'll take that."

"All right." She rose. "I'll put on my face," she

said. She watched him prowling around the room. He seemed too big for walls ... he looked uncivilized. She put her arms around him.

"Barry, it will be all right," she said.

He shook her off. "Be yourself. If you break something, it will show where it's been mended. That's not the way I want it."

She said, "You can always tell the truth; that I threw myself at you."

"There's more to it than that. I set myself up as a target. Out of curiosity, and perhaps vanity. A man doesn't stop being curious or vain because he falls in love and gets married. She's a child, I tell you ... I thought she'd outgrow it. Most people do. You did, I suppose, when you were twelve. What a god-damned fool I am; I don't *want* her to grow up ... except in her own time and her own way. She hadn't much childhood ... not the right kind ... in a way, she found what she'd missed, with me. I can't explain that; you wouldn't understand, anyway."

"Oh, snap out of it," said Val; "she's so crazy about you that you can commit murder and get away with it."

"I have, in a way, and I didn't get away with it. You and your frustrations!"

She said coolly, "Okay, blame it on me. But

you didn't make it too difficult."

"Check," said Barry. "For a man in his right mind, and in love with his wife, runs away from his curiosity and his vanity."

He stopped prowling. He took her by the shoulders and shook her hard. Her swollen eyes blazed, her hair fell about her face. He said, "Suppose you tell the truth. You don't want me, Val . . . not in the sense you tried to put over, just before Abby came in. You don't want any man. You never have. It's all window dressing; the come-and-get-me . . . the sultry stuff. Why in hell don't you go into the movies? You could put it over. They'd call you . . . The Promise."

"Let me go."

"Sure." He did, so abruptly that she nearly fell. He said, "Your marriage must suit you. You don't even have to put on an act. That's what got me, when I first knew you. I wasn't *sure*; I thought, I'd like to be . . . Then I married." His harsh voice broke. "And after that, there you were again, so I kept on wondering."

She said, "You've no right. . . ."

"Suppose Abby hadn't come in? What then? Thanks for the consolation, darling, and shall we catch the train? Perhaps, next week, when you're in town I can get down. Abby will be busy with her hospital work and her father . . . That's it, isn't it? The Promise. Only you wouldn't keep it . . . short of an altar. And you're married to a lot of money and a lot of paintings. You don't want to lose them. I'm not so safe an investment. So, what does it all mean?"

She said, "I won't listen. And I despise that old man. He makes my flesh creep."

"Has he ever been close enough?"

She said furiously, "I — I said I love you. You might have —"

"Never," said Barry. "I might have found out, in my own way, what makes you tick, or that you don't tick at all. But that hasn't anything to do with love . . . you wouldn't know that."

She said, "Neither would Abby."

"She might," said Barry, "someday. Find your things, we're getting out of here."

"My face —"

"The hell with your face," he said.

Abby caught her train. The taxi driver looked at her and thought. Never mind the cops or the tires. He got her to the station. She ran through the gates, swung herself on the last car, and the conductor put out his hand . . . the train had begun to move. "Hey, lady," he said, "take it easy."

She sat on a dusty red-plush seat and shared

it with a woman and an agile child who swiveled on his mother's lap, to put sticky, exploring fingers on Abby. She did not notice him or the country through which she passed. She did not think, or plan. She sat there, shaking inside, her mind light and unpredictable as a feather in the wind.

After a while the woman and child got off, climbing past her. The little boy said in a voice like a bird's, "What's the matter with the lady, mom, can't she move?"

No. She did not slide over to the window. She sat as if the others were still there, on the very edge of the seat. The place by the window remained vacant.

At Fairton she rose. She had wondered about that, briefly. Could she get off at Fairton, or not?

She got off and Morton was there with the station wagon. His face was indifferent, regarding her. He asked, "Didn't Mrs. Wallace and Mr. Lambert come up too?"

"No."

He chewed that over in his mind, driving home. It would make table conversation. Mrs. Renning liked a bit of gossip ... "Gets off the train looking like death, like she was walking in her sleep. I asks her, perfectly natural and civil, was Mrs. Wallace and Mr. Lambert with her. No, she says, just like that. I said something, driving back, about the stuff on the radio . . . Do you think the war's really over, I asked her? She didn't answer . . . I wonder what gives?"

23

Abby found her father in his library. He looked up as she came in. He asked, "Abby, you look tired — did you have a successful day?"

"Very successful," she said.

She began to laugh. Her laughter was rough and high in her throat; it brimmed from her eyes, laughter fluid as tears.

"Abby!"

He rose, and came toward her. He asked, "What is it? Abby, stop . . . at once."

She said, still laughing, "I can't."

He slapped her hard, across the face. The prints of his fingers remained. Abby stopped laughing, but the tears slid slowly down her face. She looked, he thought, detached, as plain as he had ever seen her, since her childhood. But alive, somehow, alive.

He went to a small cabinet, poured a measure of brandy. He said, "Drink this. Drink it, Abby, at once. There's no use calling the servants . . .

or Barry . . . Where is he, by the way?"

She drank and the good fire was in her throat and in her stomach and briefly the shaking stopped. The tears stopped. But they were there; someday she would have use for them, she thought, not now.

She said, "I bid in the Breughel and the Corot . . . under your figure. But the Monet —"

He said, "Never mind the paintings. Where are Valentine and Barry?"

Abby slid herself against the back of the chair, and looked at him, her eyes too wide. She said levelly, "As far as I know, in my apartment."

"What are you trying to say?"

She answered docilely. "After the auction I had over an hour. I didn't feel well. I went to the apartment . . . rather than try to shop."

He said impatiently, "Well?"

"Val was there," she said, as a child recites a lesson. There was no expression in her voice. But her face was strange to him; a face he had never seen. "And Barry. They were sitting on a couch . . . Val had been crying. Her lipstick was all over . . . on the edge of the highball glasses . . . on Barry —"

He said reasonably, "Abby, control yourself . . . there may be an explanation."

She said, "You are Val's husband. Do

you think there is one?"

"My dear, I am sure of it." He was solicitous, undisturbed. This troubled her, vaguely. It was out of drawing. But she didn't care. She looked down at her fingers laced together.

Her headache was worse; and the sick, swirling sensation had returned.

Wallace said, "You look very pale. Why not go upstairs and lie down? I'll have Mrs. Renning send up a tray. Surely Barry and Valentine will be on the next train . . . we can discuss this then, together."

"The next train? I don't want to see them . . . I —"

He said, "You won't have to until you wish. Go upstairs, get into bed, have something to eat."

She shook her head, swallowing. And Wallace asked, "There was a scene — at the apartment?"

His voice was quiet; and his eyes eager. But she did not look at him.

She said flatly, "I didn't make one — I was just — sick."

"Sick? Literally? You mean, nauseated?"

She said, "I'd eaten in a hurry . . . something bad, I suppose."

Wallace said, "I'll call Lansing and have him look you over. Have you considered another possibility?"

She did not reply. He went on. "Perhaps you are pregnant. It might also account for your — emotional disturbance."

"No," she said, with tired violence. But she was thinking of something else. The train. Any train that might bring Val and Barry back. She rose and pushed back her chair.

"I won't stay here," she said.

"Where will you go?"

"I don't know."

He asked, "What are your plans?"

"I just want to get away," she said.

Wallace took the house phone, and spoke into it. He said, "Find Morton, have him bring the station wagon."

He asked, "If you have no plans, have you money?"

"Enough." She stood looking at him. She said, "You don't believe that I saw anything —"

"Of course," he said. "It isn't, however, what you saw but what you read into it: I am not inimical to the idea of a break between you and Barry. In fact, I am so agreeable to it that I lean backward, to be fair. I told you once that you need not come to me if you found you had made a mistake. I retract that. If, on mature consideration, you wish a divorce, it can be quietly arranged, that is, if Barry will not contest it. If he does, that will be another matter. You understand that the grounds would have to be quite conventional: cruelty, desertion. . . ?"

She was walking out of the room, out of the house. Let her go. She would return. Where would she go? he speculated. Her apartment, if unoccupied? But she wouldn't be sure of that. Madge Duncan's apartment? It was staffed, it would not be extraordinary if she thought of going there. Or if the situation seemed too delicate, a hotel for the night.

He spoke into the house phone again. "Have Morton report to me before he takes Mrs. Lambert to the station," he said.

He thought, She'll be packing a bag.

She was not; it did not occur to her. She went out, saw the station wagon roll up, and got in. Morton came around to the door. He said, "I have to see Mr. Wallace first."

The initial warning of caution crept into her mind. She sat holding her purse. Where was she going? How? She knew where, on inspiration. She opened the purse and counted the money. She had to use it, there was no other way.

Morton came back and Abby said, "The railroad station. The northbound platform."

He waited while she was in the station. If she came out and saw him, he could say he was waiting for Mrs. Wallace and Mr.

Lambert. It was the truth.

She saw him, through the window. She went back to speak to the stationmaster. She had known him all her life. She said, desperately, "Mr. Elder —"

When he looked at her over his glasses, she went on: "Morton is outside. He may come in later and ask you where I went. I'd rather you didn't tell him . . . or anyone." She repeated, "Anyone."

Elder regarded her. Pretty thing; she looked peaked. He knew Hop Morton. He'd never liked him; few did. He thought tolerantly, Had a fight with her husband, maybe. Well, they'll make up. Marry in haste, he thought, that's what I always say.

Aloud he said briefly, "I won't tell anyone. Unless they come with a badge and make me."

His granddaughter used to play up at the Wallace place sometimes when his son was day gardener there. Morton had lied him out of his job.

She said uneasily, "Is it long before the train —?"

Elder said, "Coming in about now. You won't have an easy trip, though, and you don't look good."

"I'm all right."

The train came in. A local as far as the town

311

beyond Fairton, then an express. She saw them down the platform. Barry . . . Val. They didn't look toward her. She felt her knees shake. She got in, and said breathlessly to the conductor, "Is there a chair car?"

There was, but the seats were taken. He might do something for her later . . . where was she going?

She told him. And he advised her, "You'd better go into the diner now, miss . . . you have to change pretty soon."

But her hands were cold, her head was hot, the thought of the diner made her sick. "I'll just stay here," she said faintly.

Barry raced up to Morton. He said, "Mrs. Lambert came in on the five-o'clock?"

Morton answered, savoring the moment. "Yes, sir. But she just left on your northbound. I saw her," he said.

"Northbound?" Barry stared at him. "Are you crazy?"

"No," said Morton, annoyed. "Mr. Wallace told me to ask where she took her ticket to, at the station."

"I'll do any asking," said Barry, and went in. The waiting room was small, it smelled of dust, smoke and people. The stationmaster was closing up for a couple of hours. Barry pounded on the wooden shutter and it opened. Elder regarded him mildly. He said, "I'm going home, Bud, no train for a spell."

Barry said, "My wife . . . she just took the northbound train. Where did she go?"

"Don't believe as I know your wife."

"You know her," Barry contradicted. "Abby . . . Abby Wallace."

"Oh, her." The old man shook his head. He said, "Dave's left."

"Dave?"

"The other man. Might be he sold her a ticket . . . I wouldn't know."

He banged the shutter across. Val opened the waiting-room door. Val cried, "Are we staying here all night?"

When they reached the house Wallace was waiting for them in the drawing room. He looked from one to the other. Val had repaired the damage to her face but her eyes were reddened. He asked solicitously, "Have you had dinner?"

"We have not," Barry was shouting again. "Where's Abby, what happened? Morton told me she got on our train, headed north. The old fool at the station wouldn't tell me where she'd gone. Said he hadn't sold her a ticket."

"Perhaps he didn't," said Wallace mildly. "And she didn't take me into her confidence.

I'm afraid I gave her the idea that you might be in on this train. She probably went as far as Longfield where she could wait for a train back to New York. If she saw you and Valentine on the platform, she may go to her apartment; or, as an alternative, to your mother's."

Val said, "I'm going to my room. Where Abby goes is not my —"

"Shut up," said Barry, and Wallace raised his eyebrows. He said sharply, "This is my house, Barry. And that's a curious tone to take to my wife."

Barry said, "The hell with that. I'm going to find Abby and shake some sense into her."

Her father said, "She didn't look as if she could weather a shaking . . . she returned from town to me." His voice rose a little. "She reported the situation in which she found you and Valentine . . . I haven't heard your side, of course. I would be glad to hear what you have to say."

"Barry," began Val.

He looked at her. He turned to Wallace and said, evenly. "Val phoned me. She said she had to see me. She said she was beside herself. She suggested the apartment, knowing that Abby was at the auction. Like a damned fool I met her there."

"And?"

Barry shrugged. He said, "All right, you asked for it. She said she couldn't stand this place or you any longer . . . she wanted out. She had said something of the sort the night of the accident. I suggested the usual means. She wouldn't consider it, then. But she changed her mind. She asked me to help her."

"How?"

"Money. She told me you give her practically no cash, simply unlimited charge accounts."

"That's right," agreed Wallace; "it's a sensible practice, with a woman."

Val cried, "If you two think I'm going to stand here — and take this . . ."

"I told her," said Barry, "I'd let her have the money. Up to that point it was all very kosher. Afterwards. . . ." He looked sickened. "It doesn't matter. It was a good act. I wasn't having any but, for the moment, it took me in."

Wallace said, "Valentine isn't going to divorce me. She doesn't want to, Barry. Do you, my dear?" he asked her pleasantly.

She said sullenly, "No."

Wallace chuckled. A detached observer would have concluded he was having a very good time.

"Unless of course her act, as you call it, had succeeded," he amended. "She's quite capable of the gesture known as the double-cross. . . ."

Val cried, "Don't listen to him, Barry. He put

me up to this . . . oh, not in so many words, he's too clever for that; but suggestions, implication. He wanted you to make love to me; wanted Abby to find out. . . ."

Barry said, his muscles very tight, "Say that again."

She said, "He hated you; he was never reconciled to Abby's marriage; he thought he'd make it fail. He married me, because he knew that. . . ."

"Valentine," said Wallace, breaking in smoothly, "has always been fond of you, Barry . . . in her way."

"A convenient arrangement," said Val bitterly: "spend his money, within limits; sit at his table, eat his food, but sleep in my own bed. I thought, Pretty soft . . . it was all right with me. I don't like Abby any better than Norman likes you . . . and when he got her back, I could get out, on my own terms."

Barry said, "You make me sick at my stomach, both of you." He turned. "I hope to God I never see either of you again. Abby and I will get along without you."

He slammed out of the room, out of the house.

"So what?" Val asked her husband. Her mouth was unsteady. "What will he do now?"

"Look for her. He'll find her, sooner or later."

"Will she believe him?"

"Possibly." He regarded her gravely. "Go up and change. I have told Mrs. Renning that dinner would be very late. Would you care for a cocktail? . . . Abby had brandy," he said conversationally. "She looked badly. She was hysterical. It occurred to me that she may be pregnant."

Val said, "If she is, then you'll never get her back. She was sick, at the apartment."

"I know." He looked beyond Val. "It is difficult to think of her. I remember her mother," he said, "her beauty obliterated her . . . value. . . ."

Val stared at him. "Sometimes," she said, "I think you're quite insane."

"No." He smiled. "Merely a perfectionist."

"I'm leaving you," she said abruptly.

"I think not. I would contest a divorce, Valentine, even if you were able to obtain the necessary funds. I could name . . . your refugee friend, perhaps? Or Serge? There are others. You shall remain here. You have not deluded me. Your affairs have their origin in vanity. You covet admiration, skate superbly on thin ice. You are too enamored of your person to permit its possession, yet too self-confident, you have not always been discreet. Certain of your admirers are in straitened circumstances and would testify for a price. Some men consider

317

such testimony an accolade. Besides, it would recompense them for — your failure to follow through. So, you'll remain with me. At my age, it cannot be for long."

She was white. She said huskily, "You'll live. Your heart is sound. Dr. Lansing told me, at the time of the accident. Barry said, on the train, that you'd told Abby it wasn't, she'd repeated that to him. Oh, your heart is bad enough . . . but not that way. I told him what Lansing had said."

"That is immaterial now." He rose. "Reconcile yourself," he advised. "You have diversions. We understand each other, and on that basis will get along very well."

"But why?" she asked, reduced to simplicity. "You dislike me . . . you always have. I know it, now."

"I have no wish to lose face," he answered. "My daughter has left me. My wife must not. Your hands are tied. You don't want a scandal. Not that you would consider your parents or this community. But you have acquired some prestige. And your only authoritative passion is for luxury. You'll remain."

She would; a young woman, with unlimited charge accounts . . . waiting for him to die, the gray, undestructible old man.

She went, without another word, in defeat

and Wallace walked through to the gallery. He stayed there, for a time, looking at his paintings. He still had them.

From his apartment Barry talked to Craig Emerson in Sea Island. He admitted finally, "You're my last chance. Have you any idea where she might have gone?"

"Yes," said Craig, "but why should I tell you? Because, I suppose, I care about her. I'll go back after a while to my job, my prospects, and that lunatic asylum. I'd like to know Abby's out of it for good. If she went north, Lambert, it was to Mrs. Gambel."

24

It was very late when Abby reached the Vermont village, off the main line. It was cold. Recently it had snowed. She asked for directions and walked the short distance to a small house on a side street. The hills beyond were darker than the night, there were stars and a ghostly church spire.

It took a few minutes to arouse Mrs. Gambel. When the lights went on and the door opened, Abby said falteringly, "I – I came –"

Mrs. Gambel was speechless with astonishment, but there was no time to consider that. Abby felt herself falling, into darkness and heat and misery. She felt arms about her; and no more. . . .

In the spare room the sun shone, streaking the counterpane. Abby wore a nightgown belonging to Mrs. Gambel. Mrs. Gambel's nightgowns were crinkled seersucker, violently colored, as practical and alluring as an egg beater. Abby was very white, but her head was clear. She listened to the doctor, who was unlike the village doctors you read about. His manner was informal as Main Street but assured as Park Avenue.

She repeated incredulously, "Just — intestinal flu?"

"That's right. Sudden, sharp, mercifully brief. The trip didn't help . . . nor your fainting spell. But you'll be all right, if you stay in bed."

She said, "I felt so ill, on the train . . . I thought, I might be pregnant . . . and I was frightened."

"You aren't pregnant," said the doctor, "but if you were, what's frightening about it? You're normally healthy. It's a natural process."

She said, as if to herself, "But it wasn't the solution."

When, downstairs, he gave Mrs. Gambel her orders, the doctor said, "All this has been complicated by some sort of emotional shock."

He looked inquiring, but Mrs. Gambel left it at that. None of his business. Abby hadn't let her call him until morning. Mrs. Gambel had put her to bed, and stayed with her for what was left of the night. Abby wouldn't remember that night. She had been half out of her mind. Last night she had slept and this was the second morning.

But Mrs. Gambel would remember. If Barry Lambert found his way here, she'd a mind to shut the door in his face.

When he came, she opened it; she saw he was as drained as a man could be and still stay on his feet.

"She's here? She must be," he said. "Where is she?"

"Not so fast," said Mrs. Gambel, "She has the flu, Mr. Lambert, and is in no condition. . . ."

But he brushed past, he was halfway upstairs, and Abby's door was open. Mrs. Gambel heard it close. She sat down, in her small parlor, to wait.

"Abby?" He sat on the bed, holding her. She was very light and had no strength, she could not free herself, if she wished. "There was nothing . . . God, I swear it. She wanted to divorce Wallace, she came to me for money. He sees to it that she has none. I thought you'd want me to, so I said, sure, we'd help. She began to cry then —" He swallowed. "Loving you as I do doesn't immunize me against looking at a pretty woman, even speculating about her. But it does, against loving anyone else as long as I live. Believe that . . . try to understand it."

She felt him close, solid, the only reality. She said, "I do, I think. I'd decided to come home to you when I was well enough. I've been lying here, thinking. My father said, he married Val to protect me. It was part of a plan – his plan – to estrange me from you, through her. I don't see it clearly yet but – was that it, Barry?"

"That's right. Val told me as much. He was there. He didn't deny it. Don't talk about it now. Later, if you wish; or never. There's only one important thing. You believe me, Abby?"

"Yes."

He said, "You don't have to see either of them again. I don't think she'll go on planning for a divorce. Maybe she never meant to. I don't know . . . as long as there's anything in it for her, she'll stay Mrs. Norman Wallace. And there's nothing wrong with his heart. Lansing swears it. That was an act, part of the pattern."

After a while she asked, "How did you know I was here?"

"I didn't. I called the hotels, Mother's apartment, from our place. And, finally, Emerson. He reminded me that once before you'd asked Mrs. Gambel to help you."

She said, "Barry I felt dreadful at the auction, and afterwards. When I reached Fairton, and told Father, he suggested that I was pregnant. I thought maybe he was right. But it wasn't the answer. If we were to have any future together, it couldn't be based on that. But I'm not pregnant," she said ... "the doctor told me ... it was just flu."

He said, "What an anticlimax!" He kissed her. "When you do have a baby, I hope it's a boy. Girls are a headache. Love me?"

"Always. Don't kiss me, Barry, you'll catch the flu."

"If I do, you'll have to wait till you can take me home. Can Mrs. Gambel put me up, in sickness or in health? We're free, Abby — we can make a good life. Even useful, perhaps. You're growing up. Not too fast, though ... I wouldn't want that."

They could talk this out afterward; all the time in the world. He thought, Nothing had been shattered ... what was mutually theirs remained whole.

She was drowsy. She said, "I feel ... new ... and so happy." The assurance she had sought and never quite found was hers, now. She was certain of it. Having found it, she would never lose it. Her eyelids closed. She said, "You *do* belong to me."

"Abby, how many times have I told you?" But she was sleeping, her pallor faintly flushed, her lips redder. The heavy golden braids were across his arm. Looking at her he said softly, with incredulity and resignation, "All right, darling — as much as any man can, to any woman, and for what it's worth — I believe I do!" *

THORNDIKE PRESS HOPES you have enjoyed this Large Print book. All our Large Print titles are designed for the easiest reading, and all our books are made to last. Other Thorndike Press Large Print books are available at your library, through selected bookstores, or directly from the publisher. For more information about current and upcoming titles, please call us, toll free, at 1-800-223-6121, or mail your name and address to:

THORNDIKE PRESS
ONE MILE ROAD
P. O. BOX 159
THORNDIKE, MAINE 04986

There is no obligation, of course.